"So . . ." His eyes blazed. "You did lie."

Sierra froze in her saddle, hands motionless. Despite her best efforts, she'd revealed what she'd intended to hide.

Adam yanked at her reins. "Get down," he ordered in a voice that stung like whiplash.

"I won't!" He was so angry, she feared he might leave her in the middle of the desert. "You have no right to judge my private affairs."

"You lied to me, lady. You smiled that pretty little smile and lied through your teeth." Adam still held the paint's reins with a clenched fist.

"If I'd told you the truth, would you have listened to my reasons for wanting to find the mine?" Sierra demanded. "Would you have taken me into the Superstitions?"

Adam swore a distinctly negative answer.

"That's what I thought. And that's why I kept quiet."

Anne Marie Duquette's first two Harlequin Romance novels were set in the Colorado Rockies, an area she knows and loves. But she's equally familiar with Arizona, the location of her third story. In fact, while living there, she became fascinated by the Lost Dutchman Mine—which actually exists and which has never yet been found. But it was during the long, evening horseback rides she and her husband took through the Arizona desert that *Adventure of the Heart* really began.

Books by Anne Marie Duquette

HARLEQUIN ROMANCE
2918—AN UNLIKELY COMBINATION
3080—UNLIKELY PLACES

Don't miss any of our special offers. Write to us at the following address for information on our newest releases.

Harlequin Reader Service
P.O. Box 1397, Buffalo, NY 14240
Canadian address: P.O. Box 603,
Fort Erie, Ont. L2A 5X3

ADVENTURE OF THE HEART

Anne Marie Duquette

Harlequin Books

TORONTO • NEW YORK • LONDON
AMSTERDAM • PARIS • SYDNEY • HAMBURG
STOCKHOLM • ATHENS • TOKYO • MILAN

ISBN 0-373-03151-3

Harlequin Romance first edition October 1991

To all my friends and relatives in Phoenix,
especially the patients and staff at the
Veterans Administration Hospital Day Treatment Center

ADVENTURE OF THE HEART

CHAPTER ONE

"HE'D BETTER BE HERE," Sierra Vaughn warned the fates that had conspired against her. She was due for a change of luck, and tired of waiting for it.

She was hungry, weary and frustrated. She'd been driving in the Arizona desert all day, the sun was about to set, and she still hadn't managed to hire a guide. This was the end of the line, she thought as she drove her rental car the last few miles to her destination. This was the last camp she'd try today. She'd had more than her fill of driving around in the middle of nowhere.

Finally the dusty road ended. Sierra glanced in the rearview mirror, her blue eyes squinting against the brilliance of the evening sun. Her reflection showed an attractive but shiny face, walnut-colored hair tangled around her shoulders, and mascara that had melted and smudged in the desert heat. She pulled a quick comb through her hair.

"The things I do for a paycheck."

But Sierra was no stranger to discomfort. Besides, a job was a job, and hers was at least interesting. Getting dirty and missing dinner were minor sacrifices, she told herself, compared with doing the work she loved.

Sierra was a historian specializing in the American Southwest. Her goal was to establish herself as a writer of popular history. She'd quickly learned it was an uphill battle. Sierra had worked hard to get her pieces published, but those triumphs were few and far between. It was a tough business to break into. It wasn't until two years ago, when she teamed up with Tony Miller, another historical writer, that she finally began to make some headway.

She and Tony had met at college, and their association, both professional and social, had lasted through their school days and after graduation. They'd worked on a number of successful articles together; this present assignment had come about when they pitched a book idea to a leading publisher of popular history.

Sierra and Tony proposed to write a history of Arizona's Superstition Mountains, focusing on the nineteenth century. This would include retracing the footsteps of Jacob Waltz, also known as "the Dutchman" of the Lost Dutchman Mine fame. The legendary hundred-year-old gold mine, located somewhere in those mountains, was still the subject of speculation and continued to draw treasure hunters. Sierra and Tony intended to capitalize on that.

Not only did the idea sell to the publisher, but they each received a generous advance. It was decided that Tony would do most of the writing, and Sierra would do most of the research and photography, which was her reason for being here in Arizona.

But unknown to Tony, Sierra had a personal stake in this assignment, too....

She left the rental car and walked toward the camp about fifteen yards ahead. The setting sun created eerie shadows in the red-gold rock of the Superstition Mountains. She paused to admire their beauty before speeding up her pace. It was getting late, and she wanted her business finished before she returned to the hotel.

A slight movement in the dusky interior of a tent caught her eye. She stopped a discreet distance away, and called out the name of her last possible hope for a guide.

"Hello? Adam Copeland?"

The stranger seemed in no hurry to answer, but Sierra knew what she'd seen. She remained where she was and waited. Half a minute later a form emerged from the tent.

"I'm Copeland," he acknowledged, making no move to come closer.

Sierra smiled a polite greeting, noting that he had black hair and bronze skin. The face before her suggested both Mexican and Indian heritage. That wasn't uncommon in southern Arizona. What *was* uncommon was the tall, rock-hard build, with lean muscle definition that few men possessed. Here was a man who worked hard and whose way of life definitely agreed with him.

Sierra observed all this with satisfaction and relief. Raised in the outdoors herself, she could spot a couch potato a mile away. This was an honest-to-goodness guide. Desperate though she was for help, she had no intention of hiring someone who was overweight or out of shape. And as an added bonus, the man looked tidy, even refined, a welcome change from most of the scruffy-looking guides she'd met today.

In spite of the unavoidable dustiness of his boots, the rest of him, from his denim jeans to his faded western shirt, was spotless. Sierra felt at a distinct disadvantage as he approached and they shook hands. She could feel the griminess of her palm grate against his clean skin.

"You must be Sierra Vaughn. I understand you're looking for a guide."

"How did you know that?" she asked in surprise.

She was also surprised that his voice had no trace of a Spanish or Indian accent, or at least a southwestern drawl; he spoke in clear crisp English that suggested a private-school education.

Adam briskly released her hand. "Via the grapevine. There aren't many of us guides for hire this time of year, and we tend to keep in touch. I hear you're pretty desperate, so I knew you'd show up sooner or later. Don't you know it's dangerous to hike during the monsoon season?"

Sierra hid her irritation at the slight to her intelligence. Obviously Adam Copeland wasn't one to waste time with the usual social pleasantries, so neither would she.

"My trip here is job-related, Mr. Copeland. I have deadlines to meet. And what do you mean, monsoon season? I thought monsoons happened only in the Orient."

Adam frowned. "You're misinformed. Southern Arizona has its own unique weather patterns. We get heavy rainfall June through August. Our desert doesn't have vegetation and topsoil to soak up all the water. We have flash floods, and when we do, the Superstitions can be deadly. That's why I'm not available now. For your own safety, I'd strongly encourage you to wait."

Sierra considered that. She didn't know about the monsoons, but she wasn't afraid of a little rain. Besides, it was only the first week of June.

"If I go into the mountains now, I'll miss the summer heat." Sierra knew that full summer temperatures in the Superstitions could reach well above 120 degrees Fahrenheit. Even now the evening desert air was still in the low hundreds. "I was told you were an excellent guide. With your knowledge of the local conditions, I'm sure we could avoid any problems."

"I'm sorry, but I'm not keen on drowning. You shouldn't be, either. If you want to come back after the summer, I'll be happy to guide you. Now if you'll excuse me, Miss Vaughn, I was just about to start my dinner."

His words were clearly a dismissal, but Sierra refused to leave. Adam Copeland was her last chance for a guide.

"Correct me if I'm wrong, but I get the distinct impression that the weather isn't the *only* reason I can't find a guide." Sierra looked at him suspiciously. "Other people who've wanted guides have been able to hire them. I know, because I've checked. I must have seen every guide for hire in this area. No one wants to take *me* on."

"I'm sure they have their reasons. I've already explained mine."

"Are the rains the only reason you won't take me into the Superstitions?" Sierra asked. "I suspect there's more to it than that."

Adam's eyes narrowed as he studied her. Sierra could tell he wasn't used to being challenged. Still, he was civil when he answered her question.

"People interested in the Lost Dutchman Mine usually get into trouble," Adam replied. "No one's found that gold for over a century, but every year crazy treasure hunters show up to try their luck."

Sierra's eyes flashed. "Is that what you've heard from your grapevine? That I'm a crazy treasure hunter? I'll tell you the same thing I told them. I'm working on a book, and my publisher wants the completed version by the end of the month. That includes photographs."

"That's what you *claim*. The question is, are you really working on a book, or is that just the story you're using to get a guide?"

"I *am* working on a book," Sierra insisted. "Tony and I—"

"Tony?"

"Tony Miller." She took a deep breath and launched into her explanation. "He's my partner. We're writing a book about the Superstitions, particularly during the time of Jacob Waltz. We've already finished the rough draft, but we need some local color. I'm here to retrace the route to the Lost Dutchman's legendary location at Weavers Needle, take some notes and pictures. I'm a legitimate researcher. I have no interest in the mine other than a professional one."

"Even if you are a bona-fide researcher..." Adam said skeptically.

"I *am!* I can prove it. I—"

"You could still cause trouble. Whenever word gets around that anyone's asking questions about the mine, gold fever starts up again. People assume you've found new clues, and we guides have to put up with the crazies who'll stream in here, looking for Weavers Needle. Haven't the others told you that?"

Sierra's look of dismay showed that they had.

"And at any rate, I'm not for hire during the monsoon season," he repeated.

"Please reconsider! I only need a week of your time, and Tony and I will pay you well. Just name your price."

"I'm not interested."

Sierra wasn't giving up. This expedition was her chance of a lifetime, a chance to make a name for herself. She needed a guide. Adam Copeland was the last name on her list, and he refused to help. But she had one last card to play.

"Well, it appears I'll just have to go into the mountains alone, Mr. Copeland. Can you at least tell me where I can find some good maps?" Maybe that would show him she was serious.

"You can't go out there by yourself!" For the first time, Adam's calm was shaken.

"I can, and I will. This project means a lot to Tony and me."

Especially me, she added silently. But those reasons were personal, so she concentrated on the practical.

"I was raised in Colorado herding cattle on my parents' ranch. I'm used to navigating large distances alone. What's more, I can read and use a compass. I'll do just fine. Now, if you'll tell me where I can buy maps and maybe rent a horse, I'll be on my way."

Sierra felt Adam sizing her up, but she refused to be intimidated. She knew that her outward appearance backed up her words. Her muscles weren't as well-defined as his, but they were strong. Her face was tanned from a life spent outdoors. The tiny crinkles at the corners of her eyes couldn't be faked. She'd earned them from years of squinting in the sun.

Adam finally spoke. "If you were as smart as you say about the outdoors, you'd realize that Arizona isn't Colorado. You may be just fine in snow country, but you wouldn't last two days alone in the desert."

"There are such things as canteens," she said sarcastically. "And as I can't find a guide, it appears I have no other choice. You were the last name on my list."

Adam sighed heavily. "It's idiotic to go into the Superstitions on your own. Can't you come back when the monsoon season is over?"

"I can't afford to wait that long! You should understand that better than anyone, Mr. Copeland. We're both self-employed. My publisher says to get the photos and final draft in by July first, so here I am. If I don't, I'll have to return my advance, which, by the way, I've already spent. What's more, I have a reputation to protect."

"Your reputation isn't going to do you any good if you're dead," he said wryly.

"I appreciate your advice, but I'm going, anyway," she retorted. "There's no point in standing here arguing. It's getting darker by the minute. For the last time, will you tell me where I can get some maps and a horse? You aren't the only one who hasn't had any dinner."

"I don't think you should go into the Superstitions alone."

Sierra exhaled on a long sigh. Goodness, but he was stubborn! "So you've said. Look, I've accepted your decision not to guide me. You'll have to accept *mine* to go in alone. If you won't help me out with information, I guess I'll just leave now. I don't want to be stuck on these dirt roads in the dark."

"You could get hurt," he warned.

Sierra blinked with surprise. Was that a note of concern in his voice? If so, she regretted even more not being able to hire him. A guide who cared more about his customers' safety than their money would be worth his weight in gold.

"I'll have to chance it. If you change your mind, let me know."

Adam peered at her closely. "I'm not going to change my mind. I won't guide during the monsoon season, and neither will anyone else. I hope for your sake you're bluffing, Miss Vaughn. I'd hate having to come after you if you're stupid enough to try this alone. I'd hate even more seeing you injured—or worse."

"I asked for your guide service, Mr. Copeland, not a rescue service. I don't plan on needing it. What's more, I don't appreciate being insulted. Now if you'll excuse me, I'd like a hot bath, my dinner and a soft bed. Good night."

Adam casually brushed an invisible speck of dust off his shirt. "You'd better leave me your travel plans. Someone should know where you are in case you get lost or hurt. It might as well be me."

"I have no intention of doing either," she said tartly. "I gave that up when I left home."

"I beg your pardon?"

Sierra was irritated at herself for bringing up her personal life with a stranger, but there was something about him that broke down her usual reserve. "Back on the ranch, one of the rules was that you never traveled alone without telling someone where you were going," she explained.

"Good rule. You didn't follow it?"

"Most of the time I did, but I resented being treated like a child. After all, I wasn't treated like a child when it came to my chores. Since I worked like an adult, I felt I should have been treated like one, and not have to answer for my every movement."

"There's nothing wrong with taking precautions for children *or* adults. I'm sure your parents were only concerned for your safety," Adam said.

"They were more concerned with whether I finished my chores," Sierra said angrily. Then she was ashamed of her outburst. "Well, that's not entirely true. I remember one time when I was ten and had gone for a long horseback ride..."

"What happened?"

"I took off one day without telling anyone. When I returned, it was long past our dinner hour. I arrived home to find a search party assembling. My father's face was white and my mother was crying. It's funny. I never thought they'd be that worried. I always thought they cared more about my work potential than me. And most of the time that's how it seemed."

"That's a harsh view to take," Adam said, giving her a strange look. "Were you punished?"

Sierra shook her head. "No, they were too happy to see me. Their being so upset was worse punishment than anything they could have done to me, anyway. I still resented the rules, but I never made that mistake again."

"Then you'll tell me where you're going."

Sierra had to acknowledge the logic and, yes, the wisdom of his words.

"I want to see the southern side of the Superstitions. I intend to take the Peralta Trail first to Weavers Needle, and then on to Black Top Mountain."

Adam's concern and kind air vanished. "Black Top Mountain isn't where the mine's supposed to be located."

"I know that."

"Then why are you headed there? What's this all about?"

Sierra sighed with exasperation. "I intend to take some photos for my own personal interest after I retrace the path of Jacob Waltz," she explained. "I'll try to make a magazine sale on my own with them. My publisher isn't interested in Black Top Mountain because that area has nothing to do with the mine's alleged location, but it's good historical material." *Maybe better than you know, Mr. Copeland.*

Adam didn't respond.

"Look, I shouldn't have to defend myself. You said you weren't interested in guiding me, remember?"

Sierra didn't like the way this conversation was going. So far, everything she'd told Adam was the truth. What she *hadn't* told him was that she *did* want to find the treasure.

She had gold fever, just as he'd accused.

Sierra once again turned toward her car, but Adam quickly intercepted her. "Perhaps I've reconsidered."

Sierra paused, and studied him in the failing light. The last orange rays of the sun intensified the bronze of his skin and reflected off the gleaming black of his hair. But the light was too dim to read anything in those dark brown eyes.

"Perhaps?" She couldn't help but get her hopes up.

"You haven't convinced me you're on the level, but I certainly don't like the idea of you out there alone. I don't need your funeral on my conscience. Tell me you're not chasing treasure, and I'll hire on as your guide."

Sierra was thrown into confusion. She needed him, yet how could she admit that she *was* chasing treasure? If only she dared tell him her reasons!

She stared at Adam. He was a total stranger, but somehow she felt he was trustworthy, the kind of man she could confide in. Did she dare tell him about her disappointments? Could she tell him how she'd loved Tony Miller, then how he'd betrayed that love? Would Adam understand that this project was her last chance to make a fresh start for herself? And that it all hinged on finding the Lost Dutchman?

Sierra hesitated. She wanted to tell him the truth. She really did. But she couldn't risk it. There was too much at stake.

"I'm just completing an assignment." Thank goodness for the dark, Sierra thought. Adam couldn't see her wince at the lie.

"Hmm." He still didn't sound convinced and for a moment Sierra felt a moment's uneasiness. She had no practice in lying. She was sure he'd seen right through her.

"I'll give you Tony's phone number if you want to call him for verification," she added quickly.

"You do that. And you can be sure I'll use it." Frowning, Adam shook his head. "All right. You win. It's against my better judgment, but...I'll be your guide, as far as Weavers Needle, anyway. If the weather holds up, I may even take you to Black Top Mountain."

"I told you I'm not worried about the rain," Sierra insisted.

"I am," he replied grimly. "The Peralta's a canyon trail. Weavers Needle and Black Top Mountain are both in East Boulder Canyon, and the last place I want to be during monsoon season is on low ground. However," he said, apparently relenting, "if I can take you there, I will."

"Really?" Relief flooded through her, along with an unexpected feeling of pleasure. Although she would have gone alone if necessary, she hadn't looked forward to the prospect.

"Yes, really. But I want you to understand something. I'm not condoning what you're doing. I think it's reckless and foolhardy. But I will take you into the Superstitions."

"Thank you," Sierra said gravely. But then something forced her to ask, "If you're so against this, why do it?"

Adam thought about that a moment. "Maybe I've made myself responsible for your safety." He shrugged. "Maybe I find you a hard woman to ignore."

"Oh." She felt a tingle of pure happiness. "Well, I do appreciate it."

Adam nodded. "I'll pick you up tomorrow morning at eight. That rental you're driving isn't made for dirt roads. Turn it in if you want. Do you have your own gear?"

"I have a backpack and canteen, and I'm all set for clothes, but I'd planned on renting everything else." Sierra could barely restrain her excitement.

"I can provide your gear and mount for the week it'll take you to complete your research. Research *is* all you plan on doing, isn't it?"

"It is." The lie didn't come any easier the second time. In fact, it felt worse, because he'd agreed to help her despite his serious misgivings.

"For your sake, I hope so." His voice cut the desert air like a blast of arctic wind. "Because if you've lied to me, if you do have gold fever, you're on your own."

Again Sierra was glad of the darkness, which hid her guilty blush. Still, her voice was firm as she retorted, "You have nothing to worry about. I'll be at the Saguaro Inn. It's half an hour west of here."

"I know where it is."

"I'll see you at eight, then. Good night, Mr. Copeland. And thank you."

She walked toward her car, aware that he was watching her. She climbed inside and fumbled for her keys, feeling distinctly uneasy. But she should have been feeling satisfied, pleased, delighted—after all, she'd hired a guide, was ready to start work and was finally headed for a meal and a good night's sleep.

But she found herself remembering the steel in Adam Copeland's voice as he'd said, "If you've lied to me..."

Sierra shivered, and turned on the ignition. She'd have to make sure Adam never found out she'd done just that....

LATER, IN THE WARMTH of the hotel bath, Sierra's uneasiness returned. What would Adam Copeland say if he found out he had, indeed, been hired by a bona-fide treasure hunter? She worked the washcloth over her legs, absently cleansing away the last of the day's grime. Years of working on her parents' cattle ranch had produced the wiry strength that her feminine curves couldn't quite disguise. You didn't grow up feeding cattle and roping cattle and herding cattle without becoming strong. Even now, seven years after leaving home and that dreadful way of life, her lean body still bore its marks.

And so did her heart. It wasn't the actual ranch life that Sierra despised so much, although heaven knew she'd worked like a drudge. What she hated was the emotional climate that existed on the Vaughn ranch. Even as a child Sierra had longed to escape. All that was talked about was the stock, not the people. People were just an extension of the ranch, the cattle's caretakers. Her father, a stern and silent man who lived and breathed cattle, truly fit the title of stockman, as did her five older brothers.

Sierra's mother had been ranch-born and -raised herself, and while she wasn't as cattle-minded as the

Vaughn men, she couldn't enforce Sierra's pleas to the family not to treat her as a ranch hand.

Sierra's brothers made fun of her "high and mighty notions," while her father couldn't understand her distress. The young Sierra soon learned that no one would take her seriously unless she worked as hard as the rest of the family. Then they assumed that she was like them, and being a skilled rancher was all she needed to make her happy. It was a no-win situation.

Sierra grew up wanting one thing—escape.

She'd longed for the day when she could leave behind for good the Vaughns' strict and thankless life, with its early mornings, late nights and the never-ending chores that filled all the time in between. Sierra never had a minute to call her own. In the meantime, she'd prayed for a sign that she was loved for more than just her ability to sit a horse and rope a steer. That absence of emotion hurt more than the hard work ever did.

She'd been afraid her family would never see that she didn't fit in. When she announced she wanted to go to college and move away from the ranch, Sierra had expected resistance from her parents. But they'd willingly funded her college education, a fact that still surprised her. She hadn't wasted any time trying to figure it out. Instead, she'd rushed to pack her bags and catch her bus. She'd never looked back.

She'd opted for a degree in history, which had always appealed to her. After all the uncertainty in her own life, Sierra appreciated the certainty of the past. At least it wasn't confusing like the present, or murky like the future.

Sierra stepped out of the hotel tub and dried herself, still deep in thought. She slipped into a cool cotton nightgown and slid under the sheets. As far as her career was concerned, leaving the ranch had paid off. She managed to earn a modest living and was free from a way of life she hated. Unfortunately she'd stumbled into an even more painful situation.

It had began innocently enough, when she met Tony Miller as a junior in college. Sierra had been impressed by his fervid interest in the history of the Southwest. At first they studied together, dating casually now and then. After graduation, they kept in touch and eventually started working together. Their relationship became more serious; to Sierra, Tony seemed to fill the emptiness in her heart. When he proposed last year, she'd considered herself the luckiest woman alive.

Until a routine pre-wedding medical exam changed all her plans.

"I'm...I'm what?" she'd said to the doctor in a stricken voice.

"The medical term is sterile, Miss Vaughn."

"Sterile? But Tony and I want children! Lots of children!"

The doctor couldn't possibly know that Sierra had a strong maternal streak that had surfaced early in childhood. If she wasn't mothering the kittens or the puppies, she was crooning to the new foals or calves. Her parents had tried to discourage her, especially as calves on a ranch were bred for slaughter, while the rest of the animals were working stock.

"They're not pets, Sierra," her father had explained. "You'll ruin them if you keep spoiling them like that. If you feed the kittens treats, they won't hunt the mice in the grain bins. If you let the dogs sleep inside, they can't guard the cattle. The animals belong to the ranch, Sierra. They can't ever belong to you."

But Sierra kept making pets of them, anyway. She couldn't help herself; she was an affectionate child whose busy parents didn't have time for her loving ways. The animals were her substitute family, and Sierra found that her urge to mother grew stronger with the years.

And now she'd been told she was sterile? It was like a nightmare.

"You must be wrong, doctor!" she'd said frantically. "I've never noticed any problems."

"That's why I requested those extra tests, Miss Vaughn. Let me explain those results to you again."

And he had. By the time he was finished, Sierra no longer cherished any false hopes. She would never bear a child. No amount of surgery or prayer could change that.

With a heavy heart, she'd told Tony the devastating truth. The look on his face had frightened her. Sierra knew, long before the words were actually spoken, that the wedding was off.

Tony wanted his "own children," not someone else's "abandoned babies." Adoption was out of the question for him, and so was any possibility of Sierra's becoming Mrs. Tony Miller.

That was a year ago. Sierra had survived Tony's betrayal. She was even able to accept the new fiancée he'd first sent for fertility tests before announcing their engagement. But Sierra couldn't get used to the idea of never becoming a mother. Finally she decided that, husband or not, she was going to adopt.

That decision did much to ease the pain in her heart. But there was yet another problem. Sierra couldn't adopt unless she had a steady job. The adoption agencies frowned on free-lance research work with its uneven income. That was why she and Tony were still working together. They had pitched their book idea before the breakup. Despite their differences and the awkwardness of their past, this book deal was too big to give up. And if the book was a success, she'd benefit more than just financially.

Sierra was tired of free-lancing, tired of the struggle to find steady work. But she had plans to change all that. She'd heard there was a permanent staff job coming up at *Southwest History,* a top-notch magazine she'd frequently contributed to as a free-lancer. The Phoenix-based magazine was full of glossy photographs and articles on popular historical topics, along the lines of *National Geographic.*

Since Sierra's specialty was the history of the Southwest, she'd made regular requests regarding a permanent position. A few months ago her persistence had paid off. The owner of the magazine had called. An Arizona native, he was interested in the Lost Dutchman, and he'd heard of her book project. Depending on the quality of that book, he might be prepared to offer her a job.

Sierra badly wanted that job, and she knew a way to make the book a rousing best-seller. She had to uncover more than just the Lost Dutchman's history. She had to find the Lost Dutchman itself, together with its legendary gold. The wealth meant nothing to her. In any event, the Superstitions were now a National Forest, and any gold found in them belonged to the government.

But *finding* the gold . . . If she could find it, actually find it, she'd be famous. Next to the salvage of the *Titanic,* the discovery of the Lost Dutchman Mine would be the historical coup of the century. And that meant recognition in her field, virtually guaranteeing her the staff position with *Southwest History*.

The staff writer's job meant she'd be permitted to adopt children. Her children would be free to reap the benefits of her love, something no one ever had time for on the ranch. Or, she thought bitterly as she remembered Tony Miller, off the ranch, either.

Sierra was smart, and she'd done her homework. She had a strong theory about the mine's location. After all, as a historian, she had access to old archives, archives she knew how to use. She smiled at the thought of her name on the front pages of newspapers.

Sierra would be professionally established and financially solvent. And Tony... well, Tony still didn't grasp the importance of finding the mine.

As things stood now, their book was only a rehashing of the same old facts, supplemented by new photographs and a few new theories. But with the actual discovery of the mine, their book would become something special... something to be presented to the world with pride. Unfortunately, Tony hadn't seen it that way.

"Don't be ridiculous, Sierra. The damn mine probably doesn't even exist! Besides, the publisher isn't paying us to chase after rainbows—or to waste our time. Look, I'm getting married at the end of the summer and I want this book finished as fast as possible. I want the rest of my money." Then the parting shot, "Maybe you should use *your* share to see a good psychiatrist."

Oh, how Sierra burned at that insult. She was determined to find the Dutchman for the sake of her own career, but she was equally determined to make Tony regret those belittling words. And once she'd found the mine...

Then she wouldn't ever have to work with Tony Miller again, a man who treated her as less than a woman because she couldn't bear children. A man who scoffed at her ideas. Instead of Sierra Vaughn, childless ex-fiancée, or Sierra Vaughn, free-lance researcher hustling for assignments, she'd be Sierra Vaughn, acclaimed historical writer. Sierra Vaughn, doting mother. She'd control her destiny, instead of being controlled by it.

That is, unless Adam Copeland stopped her. Sierra again felt guilty about deceiving him, especially since he seemed genuinely concerned for her safety. She wished now that she'd told him the truth. He was obviously the kind of man who'd demand honesty in a woman, and Sierra found herself wanting him to respect her.

"You aren't chasing treasure, are you?" he'd asked.

She was, though, and she knew he wouldn't like it. So she'd lied. Well, it was too late now, she told herself, uneasily pushing aside her guilt. The damage was done. She'd just have to play the scholarly type to the hilt and do her treasure hunting in secret, even if she had to do it every night by flashlight while he slept.

Somehow, someway, she'd make certain Adam wouldn't suspect a thing. If nothing else, eighteen years of ranch life had taught her some harsh lessons, and patience was one of them. Adam didn't stand a chance against that.

The treasure of the Lost Dutchman Mine, and everything that came with it, would be hers.

She was sure of it.

CHAPTER TWO

SIERRA TOOK ONE LAST LOOK around her hotel room. It was early morning, but she'd been up for hours. She'd already dressed and eaten, intending to study her notes until Adam arrived. But she couldn't concentrate. Her attention was focused more on her guide than on anything else. She decided to call the man who had recommended Adam and see what she could learn.

Fifteen minutes later she hung up the phone none the wiser. No one seemed to know much about Adam, except that he was a good guide. Sierra vowed to find out as much about him as she could. She told herself she was only interested in him professionally, but she knew that wasn't entirely true.

A knock on the door surprised her. It was nowhere near eight.

"You're early," Sierra commented as she let Adam Copeland in.

"And you're ready to go, I see," he said. "I didn't think you would be."

"Habit. Late risers always missed breakfast on the ranch. My brothers and I worked too hard to lose out on a meal." She grabbed her backpack, which contained her clothes, notebook and camera, and followed Adam outside.

"Did you turn in your rental car?" he asked.

"I took care of that last night. We can take the side door from my room. It goes right out to the parking lot." Sierra reached for her sunglasses as she felt the first full blast of morning heat. It was already in the nineties, with the blazing sun promising even higher temperatures.

"Aren't you going to check out?" he asked curiously.

"I need a place where I can keep the rest of my stuff. Also a number where I can be reached by Tony or my publisher." And the adoption agency, she added silently. She was near the top of the waiting list, and she didn't want to take any chances. "Once we're out in the desert, the front desk can take all my messages until I get back. Besides, the off-season rates are low."

"I understand. The silver truck with the cap is mine."

Adam led her to a late-model truck and opened the passenger door. But Sierra didn't climb in right away. She was getting her first really good look at his face in the uncompromising light of day. She took in the angular lines of the jaw and high cheekbones, the full yet totally male shape of the lips, and the proud carriage of the head that suggested warrior blood, both Spanish and Indian. It was an attractive face, despite the cool scrutiny in those eyes. Sierra desperately hoped her guilt wasn't written all over hers.

"Do I pass muster?" he asked after a moment.

Sierra was embarrassed that he'd caught her staring, but she managed not to blush. "I didn't get a good look at you last night."

"Neither did I," Adam replied, and now she was the one under examination. "Boots, jeans and hat. Good." Adam studied her outfit, which was similar to his. "But you should have worn a long-sleeved shirt."

"In this heat?" Sierra's fresh shirt was already sticky in places, and her shoulder-length hair felt hot and heavy, even though she'd tied it back. "You aren't wearing long sleeves," Sierra observed as she scrambled into the truck. "You don't even have sunglasses on."

Adam didn't close her door. "I never use them. Sometimes the sun heats the frames up so much they actually brand your nose. As for the shirt, I won't burn. With your skin, you will. You ought to change."

Sierra compared his dark bronze color with her lighter tanned skin. "We aren't going into the Superstitions today, are we? We'll need to get horses and supplies first. Besides, I wore short sleeves yesterday. I'm not worried."

"I'll bet you weren't outside all day, either," Adam said. "Sitting inside a car isn't the same thing as sitting on a horse."

He glanced once more at her arms. "Let me tell you how I work, Miss Vaughn. I'm very good at what I do, and I usually give good advice." His voice was casually matter-of-fact. "Unless your life is in extreme peril, I try not to be pushy. But just because I don't like playing baby-sitter doesn't mean I'm wrong. I know what I'm talking about. When your arms burn, and they will, perhaps you'll pay closer attention to me."

Adam looked at the pack in her hands. "If you have another shirt, I'd advise you to change into it before we leave the hotel."

Sierra heard the sound of authority in Adam's voice, and she acted like one who'd been ordered around all her life on a ranch. She rebelled.

"I'll be fine, Mr. Copeland. Now shall we settle on your fee, and see about those supplies?"

Adam gave her arms one last look. "It's your money, and your hide."

Finances were discussed and quickly settled. Adam took her pack and loaded it into the back of his pickup with the rest of the gear. Then he climbed in and drove off.

"Where are we headed first?" Sierra asked.

"We have to go into Apache Junction to see Weldon, a friend of mine. I board my horse at his place, and you'll need to rent one from him."

"I hope it isn't a long drive," she said with an impatient frown. "I'd like to get the supplies today, too."

Adam gave her a curious look. "You're certainly in a hurry, aren't you? Not too many people would be in such a rush to begin a hot trip into the Superstitions. And for your information, I keep a stock of supplies at Weldon's."

Sierra tried to stifle her enthusiasm, and her guilty conscience. She had lied to this man, and now she was about to do it again, actions that were totally out of character for her. But she couldn't very well tell him she was excited to begin treasure hunting, could she?

"I just worry about my deadlines, that's all," she forced herself to say. "So, how far is your friend's ranch?" She adjusted the air vent to blow the truck's air-conditioned breeze into her face.

"We're only about twenty miles away. But most of that is dirt roads, some of them pretty bad. It might take us two hours to get there. I can turn on more air if you're still hot," he offered, a luxury Sierra gratefully accepted.

"Thanks. I should have asked for air in my rental. How do you stand these temperatures?"

Adam clicked the switch up a notch and shrugged. "You get used to it. And it's not always this bad. Desert winters are actually quite comfortable. We even get an occasional frost at night."

"Oh." Sierra continued to keep her vent pointed toward her face. She knew her cheeks were flushed. The sun was blazing into the cab, and despite the airconditioning, she was hot where its rays touched her. Her bare arm, the one nearest the window, felt as if it was roasting.

"I'll stop and get us a drink," he said, apparently sensing her discomfort. "There's a gas station up ahead. What kind of soda do you want?"

"Anything, as long as it's cold."

Adam nodded, then quickly pulled over and parked. "Roll your window down. I'd leave the air on for you, but when it's this hot, you can't let it run for long when the truck's not moving. In the desert, everyone's engine overheats. I'll hurry back."

Sierra gazed at his retreating form, absently rubbing her right arm. It was now pink instead of its usual beige, and the sun threatened to turn it pinker. When Adam reappeared with a can of ginger ale, she thanked him and immediately held it against her skin, unopened. The cool aluminum felt blissful, and she rolled the can up and down her arm before she realized that Adam was watching. She stopped abruptly and yanked open the tab, then took a long swallow, hoping to draw attention away from her burn.

She should have taken Adam's advice, she thought, but it was too late now. Any moment he would say, "I told you so."

Adam said nothing. Instead, he went around to the back of his truck where all their gear was stowed. Then he came around to her door, pulled it open, and placed her pack on her lap.

"If you go to the ladies' room and change, I'll promise to pretend that putting on a long-sleeved shirt was all your idea. Is it a deal?"

Sierra nodded as he carefully took her soda so she could lift her pack. When he held out his hand to help her out, she was surprised at the gesture. Such social niceties were obviously natural to him, but seemed out of place in a desert gas station. Still, her hand felt pleasantly at home in his.

"I'll be right back," she said, more flustered by his touch than by her sunburn.

Inside the ladies' room, she quickly found a western-style long-sleeved shirt and changed, then hurried back to the truck with her gear.

"That was quick." Adam gave her back the soda, then started the truck.

"Another thing I learned on the ranch. The slow hands got assigned the dirtiest jobs and the worst horses."

Adam grinned, easing the truck out of the gas station and back onto the highway. Sierra tucked the pack at her feet and finished her soda. The sun still glared through the windows, but with the air-conditioning and her long sleeves, she was fairly comfortable.

"Thanks for the soda—and the advice about the shirt. I really do know better," she said ruefully. "It's just that I've gotten used to being on my own. I don't take orders very well."

Adam smiled slightly. "I thought we agreed to pretend that changing was your idea."

"I can admit when I'm wrong. Though I hate doing it." Sierra smiled back. "I always did."

"At least you realize it," Adam said, his voice amused. "That's half the battle."

"I not only realize it, I work on it. I wouldn't be a very good researcher if I didn't. And speaking of research—" Sierra took out her notebook and pen from her backpack "—do you mind if I ask you a few questions about the Lost Dutchman Mine?"

Adam's smile instantly vanished. "I thought you just wanted to retrace the alleged route and take photos."

"I do, but I want to get some local opinions about the mine. Which theory do you support about its origin?" Sierra asked.

"I'd have thought you and your partner would already have that information." Adam stubbornly refused to answer the question. "You said you had the rough draft finished."

"We do, but we need some local flavor. It'll contrast nicely with my archival research." Sierra refused to put away her notebook. "I didn't think you'd mind answering a few questions."

"I'd rather ask you the questions," Adam replied. "I like to know a bit about my clients before any expeditions. Are you married?"

"What kind of question is that?" Sierra challenged. "Why don't you ask about my education or my professional background?"

Adam grimaced. "Believe it or not, I once had a jealous husband accuse me of trying to steal his wife because I pitched my tent too close to theirs. It ruined the whole trip."

"I see." Sierra was piqued to find that his question was purely job-related. "Well, I'm single. You?"

Adam looked sideways at her, one eyebrow lifted, before turning his attention back to the road.

"Fair's fair," Sierra insisted. "I don't want a jealous wife accusing me of trying to sneak into your tent. So, are you?"

"I have no wife, no girlfriend. The life of a desert guide doesn't seem very attractive to women. Since you don't have a husband, is there a boyfriend I should worry about?"

Sierra thought of her sterility, and how Tony had reacted to it. "Right now, the idea of a steady man in my life holds little appeal."

"I see. Then I can assume you don't have any children?"

"No, not yet. But I will someday. I plan to adopt one soon, I hope." Sierra's voice grew soft. "I passed my final interview with an adoption agency in Denver last month. I could become a mother any time now." She didn't add that approval was conditional on a guaranteed income—the income *Southwest History* could provide.

"Adoption? You?" Adam's voice was abrupt, even harsh.

"Why not? There's nothing wrong with being a single parent. Just because I'm not married doesn't mean I shouldn't be a mother."

"Children should have the benefit of a mother *and* a father," Adam said.

Sierra crossed her arms over her chest. She'd come up against this attitude before, especially from her parents when they'd first heard of her plans. She wouldn't be baited.

"I agree, in principle. But I refuse to marry just so the children I want will have a father. I won't settle for just any man. I want someone I'm deeply in love with, who's willing to accept me as I am, flaws and all."

Especially the physical ones. "I haven't found him yet. I thought I had, but . . ." Her voice trailed off.

Adam glanced at her, but Sierra refused to elaborate. "I don't know if I'll ever find him," she said instead. "In the meantime, I'm not getting any younger, and I want children. Married or not, I think I'd make an excellent mother. And I don't see what this discussion has to do with your being my guide."

"It has nothing to do with my being your guide. It has everything to do with the fact that I was raised in an orphanage."

Sierra's jaw dropped. "You were raised in an orphanage?"

"Yes. My mother was poor, unmarried and pregnant. She left me at the orphanage, then later died of malnutrition-related causes. I never knew who my father was."

"I . . . I'm sorry."

"There's no reason to be. Contrary to popular opinion, being an orphan doesn't mean I was Oliver Twist. I was raised in a Catholic orphanage in Mexico. It was run by American missionaries, though of course some of the nuns were Mexican. They saw to all our needs. When I was old enough, they even sent me to college here in Arizona."

Sierra nodded. That upbringing explained his carefully enunciated English.

"You were never adopted?" she asked curiously.

"I had a trial adoption once, by a single woman. Like you. It only lasted six months. Even though I was on my best behavior, she returned me to the orphanage. The worst part was that I had grown to love her during that time. So you can understand why I'm a firm believer in two-parent adoptions. It increases the odds for success.''

''I see. And I'm very sorry.'' She ached with sympathy for him, but wasn't about to explain why there probably wouldn't be a husband in her life.

''Well, you haven't been offered a child yet,'' Adam said, with unmistakable relief.

''Sometimes those waiting lists take forever,'' she replied. ''So tell me, what did you major in?''

Adam graciously accepted her obvious desire to change the subject. ''Music. It seemed a logical choice. I was always interested in it, and from the age of about twelve, I was the organist for our church.''

''How did you end up as a guide?'' Sierra asked.

''By default, I suppose.''

''But surely you could have tried to break into the music world,'' Sierra persisted.

''I did. In fact, I was a sought-after studio musician, with more work and money than I knew what to do with. With my keyboard skills, it was easy to move into playing the big high-tech synthesizers. I did a lot of background fill for rock groups.''

''You?'' Sierra couldn't hide her surprise. ''You don't look—'' She caught herself, not wanting to be rude, but Adam finished the sentence for her.

''The type? Well, I suppose I wasn't. I love music, but being a professional musician was hard on me. I wasn't used to the city after growing up in the desert. Talk about the proverbial fish out of water. All those crowds and noise and traffic were—'' he winced at the memory ''—painful, to say the least. People seemed to be everywhere, intruding on my privacy, wanting things from me I wasn't willing to give. Couldn't give. Especially the women,'' he said in a low voice.

"I guess life in the fast lane wasn't for you."

"No. All I wanted was my music. But it became harder and harder to deal with that kind of life."

"So you left?"

"Yes. The pressures of city living became so great that I lost all pleasure in working. That was the biggest shock. It meant I had to rethink my values, my priorities."

"Being a guide is obviously a simpler way of life. But you can't tell me it's easier. And it certainly can't pay much."

Adam stared straight ahead at the road. "It doesn't. But I made a lot of money when I was a studio musician. And I take other jobs during the off-season. I work the rodeos, and train and haul horses. I drive machinery during harvest season."

"Harvest season?"

"Cotton harvesting. Arizona harvests a huge crop every year, just as the Indians did centuries ago. The job's hard, but the pay's good. And it doesn't cost me much to live. I put most of it in the bank."

"But to go from being a university-trained musician to doing physical labor... Don't you miss your music?"

"I don't miss it, because I never gave it up," Adam said with a smile, apparently not annoyed by Sierra's numerous questions.

"But you can hardly haul an organ around the desert."

"Right now my specialty is the reed flute."

"Reed flute? Not the metal?"

"I'm proficient on that, but I prefer working with a flute that's hand-carved from wood."

Sierra frowned. "Isn't it hard to build up any kind of repertoire with one of those?"

"Not at all. You see, many Indian tribes of the Southwest used carved flutes for their songs. The problem is that their music's dying out. The songs are usually passed down from generation to generation. With so many younger Indians leaving for the cities, the songs aren't being passed on. And the older generations aren't willing to have their music recorded, since much of it has religious significance."

"So you've been trying to learn the songs yourself?" she guessed.

"Yes, as many as I can, with as many tribes as possible. The Pima, Maricopa and Apache are the traditional occupants of the Superstitions, and there's a smattering of Hohokum. I have many friends among the desert people, and they teach me their songs. They trust me," he said simply. "I not only learn the songs, I write them down. I've been working on my collection for years."

"What a wonderful way of keeping in touch with your music! Still, it seems too bad that you'll never have a successful career as a musician."

"Success is measured in different ways, Miss Vaughn," he told her quietly. "I never measured mine in bright lights and big paychecks."

Sierra squirmed. That was exactly how she defined success. Suddenly she felt foolishly gauche, and she tried to talk her way out of it.

"But don't you wonder how your life would have turned out if you'd stuck with your career? I sometimes wonder how my life would have turned out if I hadn't been raised on a ranch."

Adam shrugged lightly. "I don't think in those terms. I don't resent my background, or the way I grew up. I have fond memories of the people who raised me and the children I grew up with."

"It sounds like you had a happy childhood."

The happiness in Adam's eyes faded. "As long as I remained in the orphanage, I did. It was the time I wasn't there that was hell."

"You're referring to your trial adoption," Sierra said quietly.

"Yes. The trauma of that failure was one of the reasons I was never adopted. The very thought of leaving the orphanage again was too upsetting."

"It must have been rough on you."

Adam's face became closed and tight. "Save your sympathy. As an adult, I don't need it. As a child, however, it was a different story. It's a terrible thing to build a child's hopes, and then dash them to the ground. I'm only telling you this because I want you to reconsider your plans to adopt. Don't make some child suffer what I went through."

"I'm not like those people. I'd never do to a child what was done to you. Never!"

Sierra drew in a shaky breath. What Adam must have suffered! To be rejected like that. To spend his life belonging to no one. At least she belonged to a family, even if they'd forced her to live a life she hated.

"I know you mean that now, but things can change and so can you," Adam said.

"I'm not going to change my mind about this," Sierra replied firmly. "Besides, I've planned for all contingencies."

"You don't know what the future holds or how your circumstances might change. And if you can't adopt, then what? You don't strike me as the kind of woman who would get herself pregnant without being married."

"I'm not." She'd never be pregnant, period.

"Well, then your future child may end up with both a mother *and* a father, right?"

Sierra shook her head. "It'll never happen," she declared. "And that's all I'm going to say on the matter."

Adam gave her an assessing look, but showed no more inclination to talk, and Sierra pretended an interest in the scenery as they drove. She wondered why a man who had such strong feelings on family relationships remained a solitary desert guide. Obviously his adoptive mother's desertion had deeply affected him. It almost seemed as if he was afraid of forming ties with anyone. His name fit him, Sierra decided. Adam—the solitary man.

"Are we almost at the ranch?" she asked much later.

"Yes. And it's not much of a ranch." Adam's manner was polite, although a bit stiff. "Weldon only keeps half a dozen horses besides mine, and a few chickens. He knows we're coming, but he may not be around. He hires out for work when the horse-rental business is slow."

Sierra nodded her understanding. After a few minutes, Adam turned off the highway onto the frontage road, and then onto another dirt road. They bumped and jolted along in the dust, as a few ranch buildings came into view.

"Here we are." Adam parked the truck near a weathered wood corral in front of an even more weathered barn. There was a small brick house, too, its color faded to a dull rust.

Sierra opened the door of the truck and slid out. The hot air hit her like a blast furnace. She adjusted her hat against the glare of the sun and squinted into the distance. To the east, the muted bronze of the Superstition Mountains was discernible through a haze of dust. The monochrome beige of the sand was broken up by the vivid green of the saguaros and the dull brown of creosote bushes. A few scraggly mesquite trees survived next to the horses' water trough, and the half-dozen mounts penned in the corral were crowded, motionless, under their scanty shade.

Sierra reached into her pocket for her sunglasses. Her hat brim offered no protection from the fierceness of the sun.

"Why aren't the horses in the barn?" she asked. The barn had no doors, and the animals could enter or exit at will.

"It's probably stifling in there." Adam checked the water level of the trough and frowned, then turned on the tap full blast. The horses shifted a little at the smell of fresh water, and one bold brown-and-white paint shoved his nose under the pouring stream and snorted.

"I don't think Weldon's here. The trough's low, and I don't see his truck. Let's go in the house."

He patted a roan Appaloosa stallion that Sierra guessed must be his own horse. Adam waited until the trough filled, then shut off the spigot. To Sierra's surprise, he took her arm and tucked it inside his.

"Stay close. Weldon owns a mutt that can be as mean as a hangover."

Sierra looked furtively around. "Great."

She found her second physical contact with Adam just as pleasant as her first, back at the gas station. For the first time since Tony, she was aware of herself as a woman. She wished she hadn't angered Adam with her stand on adoption. Under other circumstances, they might have been friends. Maybe more than friends . . .

Sierra tried to ignore the touch of Adam's body, but that was as hard as trying to ignore the sun beating down on them. Her shirt was already damp, and the sweat ran freely down her face and neck.

They were within a few steps of the house when a flash of brown charged them from under the wooden porch steps. Sierra instinctively flinched, but Adam's firm, "Down, Sin!" had the dog pausing, then actually wagging his tail.

Sierra breathed a sigh of relief, then unclenched her fingers from Adam's arm. "Whew. He took me by surprise."

"Sin does that to people." Adam reached down to stroke the shaggy brown head. "You should make friends with him."

"I'll pass for now." Sierra had been around dogs too long to mistake the mistrust in the animal's eyes. "He doesn't look too friendly just yet. What's his name? Sinbad?"

"No, just Sin." Adam straightened and walked onto the porch to try the front door. It was unlocked, and he motioned Sierra into the house. "He's part dog, part coyote. There's a lot of that combination in Arizona. I found him as a pup one day, tangled up in some barbed wire, and I brought him to Weldon. The dog was a mess. Weldon took one look at him and said, 'This mutt's ugly as sin.' The name stuck."

Sin wagged his tail at the sound of his name and apparently took it as an invitation to follow them in. The door opened into a kitchen on the right and a tiny parlor on the left. It was cool inside from a window air-conditioning unit, and Sierra sighed in relief.

Adam found a note on the battered kitchen table and read it aloud. "'Out on a job. Help yourself to what-ever. Be back late tonight. P.S. Would you water the horses? I already fed them double rations.'"

"It's just the two of us, then. In that case..." Adam tossed down the note and walked purposefully toward the air conditioner. "This goes off."

"What did you do that for?" Sierra asked in dis-may. "It's hot out there!"

"It's even hotter in the Superstitions. If you can get through today without passing out, you might just sur-vive in the mountains. Consider this a test period."

"Thanks a lot." Sierra took off her hat and fanned her face with it. "And if I feel I don't need the test?"

"You're always welcome to look for another guide," he said easily. He opened the refrigerator to pull out two cans of soda. "Here, sit down and have a drink."

Sierra took one last look at the silent air conditioner, then did so. She'd be foolish not to go along with Adam's wishes, at least for now.

"What other little tests do you have in store for me?" she asked. Patience, that was the key, she told herself.

"Well, now that you mention it... Before it gets any hotter, I thought I'd see for myself just how well you ride. And perhaps a night spent under the stars wouldn't hurt, either."

Sierra frowned. "Why ride in this heat? It won't be much fun for either me or the horses. I already told you I can ride."

"Since I'm going to be risking my own skin guiding you during monsoon season, I think I'm justified in asking you to verify your riding abilities. As it is, I've already called Tony Miller to confirm your identity. When we were at the gas station," he added, obviously in response to her puzzled frown. "You think I'm overstepping my bounds?" he asked.

Sierra guiltily remembered the lie she'd told, and that tempered her answer. "I did give you the number," she acknowledged. "I didn't really expect you to call, though."

Adam ignored that. "I have to see how you handle a horse, since that's how we're going to be traveling." He shook his head. "You have no idea how many people swear they're seasoned campers when they aren't. I need my sleep. I hate having to hold hands with saddle-sore tourists afraid of the dark."

Sierra smiled with amusement. "I don't belong in that category, but don't worry. I'll agree to whatever you have in mind."

"Good." Adam grinned, and Sierra was shocked anew by the rush of attraction she felt for him. "If you're the nervous type, Sin can always keep you company in your tent tonight."

"Sin alone might make me the nervous type," she replied, but she ventured a tentative pat on the dog's head. Goodness, but he was ugly. Most of the men she knew wouldn't have bothered with a half-wild dying beast. Very few would have saved that animal, and then found it a home.

Sin thumped his busy tail on the bare linoleum, and Sierra fondled the huge ears.

"Sin's a big baby at heart," Adam said. "I'd planned on keeping him myself, but Weldon grew attached to him. Weldon's in his sixties, and he recently lost his wife to illness," he explained. "I guess he was lonely."

Weldon was lucky to have Adam for a friend, Sierra thought, instinctively feeling that once Adam gave someone his friendship, it was for life. But all she said was, "I can't see anyone arguing very hard over the ownership of this homely thing."

"Sin's a good watchdog. We have a large population of his coyote relatives around here. Thanks to Sin, Weldon's chickens have so far remained unmolested." Adam rose to his feet.

"Come on. It's hot, but it's only going to get hotter. I'll go saddle up a horse while you pitch a tent to spend the night in. Grab one of mine from the back of the truck. Meet me at the corral when you're ready."

Pitching the tent took Sierra very little time. As she stowed her backpack inside, she ruefully remembered the empty hotel room she was paying for. Still, she considered camping out in the desert a vast improvement over camping out back home. She'd always wished for warmer summers in the mountains and felt positively ice-veined in the winter. She'd discovered, too, that the towering peaks and lush evergreens of Colorado made her feel slightly claustrophobic. Here there were miles and miles of open spaces, a shimmering blue sky and a fiery sun to warm it. She vowed to make an extra effort to acclimatize. If horses and dogs with their heavy coats could adjust, so could she.

When she headed for the corral, she saw that Adam was already waiting, with Sin sprawled at his feet. The brown-and-white paint, the horse Sierra had noticed earlier at the pump, had been saddled for her and tied to the fence.

"Aren't you riding?" she asked Adam.

"No. I can watch you from here." Adam untied the paint and led him over to her, holding the reins as she mounted. "Just trot him down to the mailbox and back."

The rusty dented box was at the end of Weldon's dirt road. Riding there and back would take no more than five minutes. Sierra was suddenly suspicious.

"Is that *all?*"

Sierra knew Adam wanted to spare the horse because of the afternoon heat, but this hardly seemed much of a test. She smelled mischief, and on impulse gave Adam her hat and sunglasses after taking the reins. If this horse was a bucking rodeo ride, she wanted her vision unhampered. Adam's eyes twinkled, putting her even more on guard.

"I don't think you'll lose your seat."

"I should hope not. Step back, please."

Sierra gently pressed her heels to the horse's sides and clicked her tongue. Nothing, not even the slightest movement, occurred beneath her. She repeated her actions with a little more force. Still nothing.

"Stubborn little gelding, isn't he?" Adam remarked.

"Not for long," Sierra replied, annoyed that she'd been stuck with such a sorry mount. But she'd ridden balky mules like this back at the ranch, and she knew the cure.

Without warning, she pulled the horse's head into a tight turn with the right rein. The sudden tension of the bit wasn't painful, but it was uncomfortable, and the horse shifted his rear quarters to straighten himself out. Sierra refused to allow that to happen. She continued to keep the right rein taut, forcing the horse to scramble around in circles.

Finally she relaxed the reins and allowed the horse to align itself. Gauging the distance to the mailbox, Sierra once more kicked the horse's sides. Still no response.

"We'll have to do this the hard way," she warned the paint. Once again she forced him into circles, only this time they were tighter and faster. When Sierra finally allowed him to stop, the gelding was trembling with frustration. She rubbed his neck and gave him a few minutes to calm down.

Then she gently clicked her tongue. The paint moved forward in a straight line before she even had to touch her boots to his flanks.

"That's much better," she praised. The horse flicked his ears attentively in her direction. He was ready to please now, and it was no effort at all to reach the mailbox, do a close turn around it, and ride back to Adam.

She stopped smartly in front of him, so close that a nervous Sin tucked in his tail and retreated. Adam held his ground.

"Got any hoops for me to jump through, or am I all finished?" Sierra asked, piqued that Adam didn't look as pleased with her performance as she felt.

"Just one more thing."

Sierra sighed loudly. "Now what?"

"Take this." Adam picked up the coiled lariat hanging on a post of the corral and tossed it to her. "I want to see you use it."

"Whatever for? There aren't going to be any cattle in the Superstitions."

"You said you were from a cattle ranch. You shouldn't mind giving me a little proof."

Sierra bit her lip in anger. "You mean you want to see if I'm a weekend cowboy? If you want proof, I'll give you proof." She examined the lariat. "My backpack's in the tent. You'll find some leather gloves inside it. Would you please get them for me?''

Adam left, then came back with her gloves a couple of minutes later.

When Sierra had pulled them on, she shook out a loop before carefully coiling the lariat and positioning it in one hand.

"This horse won't spook at a rope, will he?" she wondered. "If he does, I won't get an accurate throw."

"No, he's rope broke." Adam leaned against the corral fence.

"What do you want me to rope? Another horse? A fence post?"

"Just head down to the mailbox again, then come back at a canter," he ordered. "When you reach me, you'll see your target."

"Great," Sierra mumbled as she clicked to the horse and got him into a brisk trot. "Just great. I hope this mule doesn't throw *me* when I throw my loop."

Sierra reached the mailbox, then kicked the paint into a canter as they headed back to the corral. She'd roped thousands of ornery cattle in her life. Adam Copeland's target shouldn't be any trouble at all. Her eyes were fixed on him, her roping arm ready.

The paint kept up a steady pace as he approached the corral. Suddenly Adam yanked off his broad-brimmed leather hat and threw it. The paint veered slightly in surprise, but Sierra's loop was already hissing through the air. It settled around the hat, then tightened with a flick of her wrist. Sierra slowed her horse and retrieved her line. At the end of the lariat was Adam's hat, the crown crushed in the middle where the loop held it fast.

Sierra rode toward Adam, then reined in the paint. She loosened the lariat, pulled out the hat and proudly tossed it to him.

Adam gave a low whistle. "I'm impressed. Even I can't do that, and I work the local rodeos."

"It's all in the wrist." Sierra's expression was smug. "Not one of my brothers could outrope me."

From long years of habit, Sierra recoiled the lariat, then hung it neatly on the pommel of the saddle. She watched Adam punch the hat to reform it, smoothing out the creases with strong fingers.

"Well, Miss Vaughn, it appears you're everything you say you are. We'll head out for the Superstitions first thing tomorrow morning."

CHAPTER THREE

"HOW LONG will you be staying in the Superstitions, Adam? Your usual two, three days?"

At the forest ranger's question, Adam looked up from the sign-in log.

"This isn't my usual tourist run, Jack," he explained, obviously acquainted with the ranger. "We'll be here about one week."

That was how long Adam had agreed to guide Sierra. She stood beside him, holding the horses' reins in the blessedly cool early-morning air. Sierra still couldn't believe she was actually here. It seemed that once Adam made up his mind, things moved fast.

Last night Weldon had returned home in a beat-up old truck with a bad paint job. This morning, immediately after dawn, he'd driven them to the head of the Peralta Trail, the main entrance into the Superstitions. He'd helped them unload and saddle the horses, and secure their saddlebags and supplies. Sierra had brought only the essentials for this trip, leaving her backpack at Weldon's place.

Weldon had just left in Adam's truck, taking it and the horse trailer back to his ranch. Sierra and Adam were now at the trailhead to sign in, a Forest Service requirement for anyone entering the Superstition National Wilderness Area.

"Where will you be exiting?" asked the ranger.

"Weldon plans to meet us at the First Water Trailhead with the horse trailer a week from today."

Jack nodded, and Sierra watched him make a notation in his log. Just then, the paint snorted, pawing the ground, and she tightened her grip on the reins. When Weldon had heard that Sierra could control Spot, as he called the paint, he'd immediately rented him to her at a reduced rate. Weldon said it was about time the paint earned his keep.

Adam's horse, the strawberry-roan Appaloosa, was giving her no problem. The stallion's tail swished contentedly across white flanks dotted with red, dollar-sized circles.

"Monsoon season isn't the best time of year to be in this area," the ranger cautioned. "If the heat doesn't get you, the storms will."

"I know," Adam agreed. "We'll be careful."

"You do that." The ranger wore a worried expression. "If it starts raining hard, head for high ground. We get a lot of flash flooding in the canyons."

"Thanks for the warning, Jack, but you know this isn't my first trip out here," Sierra heard Adam say.

"I don't want it to be your last, either." The ranger held out the log to him. "Here, Adam—sign. And make sure you put down Weldon's phone number."

Adam did, then held the horses while Sierra signed her name.

"Have a safe trip," were the ranger's parting words.

"We will," Adam replied. "All right, Miss Vaughn, mount up."

The paint was cooperative, standing still as she climbed into the saddle. She reached into her jeans pocket, pulled on her leather riding gloves, then adjusted the lariat she'd borrowed from Weldon on her pommel. She felt slightly silly carrying it, but ranch ways were deeply ingrained in her. Her father had always insisted she take a compass, a knife, waterproof matches and a rope when she went anywhere on horseback; he said a person could survive in the wilderness with those four things.

"Ready for the roundup?" Adam noticed her adjusting the rope. He swung himself easily into the saddle, the Appaloosa shifting from foot to foot in his eagerness to go.

Sierra pulled back her hand self-consciously and shrugged. "I'm so used to carrying one, I'd feel uncomfortable without it. I suppose old habits die hard."

Adam nodded. "We can ride side by side. The trail's wide enough. It won't start to narrow for a while yet."

Sierra spurred the gelding until he was trotting beside the Appaloosa. "It's beautiful," she said, gazing at the spires ahead of them.

"Enjoy it while you can. Once it starts getting hot, you won't want the sun in your face."

Sierra continued to tilt her head toward the sky as she rode, her cowboy hat sliding down her back until the chin tie halted its progress.

"These are nothing like the mountains back home."

"The Rockies are mostly granite," Adam informed her. "The Superstitions have feldspar crystals embedded in a granite groundmass. It's the feldspar that gives the mountains their distinctive bronze coloring."

"Did you study geology, too?" Sierra asked.

"No, music was my specialty. But I've picked up some geology here and there. The people I guide expect me to answer their questions."

"That's understandable. I appreciate any information that will help my book, Mr. Copeland."

"As long as we're on the trail, why don't we drop the formality and use first names? You can call me Adam."

"If you'll call me Sierra," she agreed. "Isn't Adam Copeland an unusual name for someone raised in Mexico?"

"Not really. The orphanage got a lot of unidentified and unnamed infants, so the nuns made chronological use of the names in the Bible. I was one of those unnamed infants. The last male name in the Bible had just been used, so they started from the book of Genesis again. I became Adam." He shrugged. "It's better than being one more Juan, or another José. As for Copeland, I was given one of the missionary nuns' maiden names—her surname before she took her religious name. That was also common practice back then."

Sierra thought hard. "What *is* the last name in the Bible?" she asked, embarrassed that she couldn't remember. Her own childhood Bible classes seemed long ago.

"Moses. A reference is made to him in the Book of Revelations."

"I didn't know that."

"You weren't raised in a Catholic orphanage, either."

Sierra couldn't think of an appropriate reply, so she said nothing. Then the trail started to narrow, and she was forced to fall behind the Appaloosa. She noticed that the land, which she'd assumed would be barren, had a fair amount of scrub and bushes—even a few trees. She hoped there would be enough for the horses to eat. An hour later, when the trail widened again and she was able to pull abreast of Adam, she asked him about it.

"They'll have to work at filling their stomachs, but they won't starve," he assured her.

"These plants aren't familiar to me."

Adam pointed them out. "The smaller brown shrubs are the creosote bushes. They're too resinous for horses to eat. Take a good sniff and you'll see."

Sierra did, wrinkling her nose as she tried to identify the unpleasant smell.

"The odor that smells like freshly coated railroad ties comes from their sap. The mesquite, on the other hand, are edible."

"Which ones are they?"

Adam pointed. "Look for the shrubs and trees with the lime-green bark. See the brown pods? They're rich in sugar, and livestock all over use them as feed."

"But won't the horses need more than that?"

"Yes, but with the monsoon season, there's enough moisture for the grasses, too. The horses will be fine, as long as we give them long picket lines to graze and move them often."

"I've never seen a tree with green bark before."

"It's an adaptation to the desert. Leaves are fragile and vulnerable, so desert trees have tough narrow leaves that don't lose a lot of moisture. The mesquite tree takes it one step further. If the heat and wind destroys its leaves, the bark can still carry on photosynthesis. The tree has a much better chance of survival."

Sierra made a mental note to record that; she and Tony wanted authenticity in their book. She also admired Adam's knowledge. Familiar with the outdoors herself, she was pleased to see that he knew the terrain. The more he knew, the fewer the risks for both of them. And the more quickly she'd finish up the work she and Tony had promised their publisher, which meant more time for her own secret work—searching for the Lost Dutchman.

"How far are we from Weavers Needle?" she asked.

"Not far. It's to the northeast—looks like a heart half buried in the ground."

Sierra shaded her eyes and stood in her stirrups. "I can't see it."

"We're not at a good angle, but I'll point it out when we get closer. It's only a day's ride away, but depending on the heat, we may need to take two. I'm assuming you want to poke around that area?"

"Yes. Weavers Needle traditionally marked the Dutchman's location, so that's where I want to concentrate. Tony specifically asked me to get lots of pictures there."

"As long as taking pictures is all he told you to do," Adam muttered.

"Tony isn't my boss," Sierra said irritably. "We're equal partners."

She always ended up researching, while Tony sat in his plush desk chair writing up her hard-earned notes, she thought with sudden resentment. Still, it kept them apart, which was something she'd come to appreciate. And generally she did enjoy her more active role. But she was looking forward to working on projects from start to finish. She'd do all her own writing at *Southwest History,* Sierra promised herself. She had only to complete the research for this book, and that would be the end of any association with Tony Miller.

"I see. So, we'll concentrate on Weavers Needle?" Adam asked.

"Only until I get everything we want. Afterward, I might want to check out some, uh, other locations."

According to her research, the traditional site wasn't where the mine was located. She suspected the Dutchman was somewhere else, near Black Top Mountain, the next landmark they'd reach after Weavers Needle. She was dying to know if the mine was where she'd pinpointed it. It made sense for the actual mine to be located somewhere other than Weavers Needle. That area had been searched with a fine-tooth comb for years, and the Dutchman had never turned up.

"Like I said before, I'm always on the lookout for new stories and research for my own work," Sierra added.

"Yes," Adam said absently. "We'll set up camp wherever we find water. Because of the rains in the last few weeks, there should be enough pockets of water for the horses. We shouldn't have to use what we're hauling for them. And speaking of the horses, I want to remind you that this isn't Colorado. They suffer from the heat just as we do, only they don't have canteens. We don't push them above a walk, and we stop as often as they need it. If Spot starts lathering heavily or suddenly slows, pull up."

Sierra damped down her excitement over the Dutchman and tried to pay attention to Adam's words. She couldn't let him guess she had gold fever.

"I will. I still can't understand why Weldon named this beautiful paint Spot," she said, making conversation.

"Weldon isn't too original with names," Adam replied. "He also has a propensity for names beginning with *S*. In fact, he found your name quite attractive. I think he plans to use it for his next hen."

Sierra's lips twitched. She was more amused than insulted. "Spot, Sin and Sierra. What a combination. I hope your horse's name is a little more original."

Adam patted the stallion's neck with an affection that Sierra found herself envying. "You're looking at

Lightning Bolt. He's the offspring of champions, and he's registered with both the American Quarter Horse Association and the Appaloosa registry.''

''He's a beautiful animal. He must have cost a small fortune.''

''If he did, he was worth it. Besides, I have little else to spend my money on.''

''But you told me you earned a good salary as a musician. Don't you have a home?''

It seemed to Sierra that Adam took a long time to study the trail ahead of them before he answered her question. ''By home, do you mean a place with a white picket fence and flowers out front?''

''Something along those lines.''

''I don't have a house. I do own about twenty acres of land out here in the desert. I'd planned on building, but . . .'' He shrugged. ''I wanted a home for my family. Since I don't have a family, I don't need a house.''

''Maybe someday you'll find a woman you want to marry. Then you'll build your house in record time,'' Sierra said.

Adam gave a wry smile. ''Perhaps. I bought the land for a future I've never realized. Unless and until that happens, it's best to leave it alone.''

Adam spoke with no trace of self-pity or bitterness, but still Sierra was prompted to say, ''I'm sorry.''

''Don't be. I have my truck, my tent and my sleeping bag. Weldon takes care of my horse, and I have an open invitation to bunk with him whenever I want.''

Sierra couldn't believe what she was hearing. ''Is that all you want out of life?''

There was the slightest hesitation. ''That's all I need.''

Sierra watched as Adam spurred his horse forward so that they were no longer riding abreast. The snub was obvious. Her inquiries had been too personal, and the easy camaraderie of earlier had changed back to a guide-customer footing. Sierra felt a stab of regret. He was good company, so different from her often-quarrelsome brothers and her self-involved ex-fiancé. More than that, she felt strongly drawn to him. He seemed to understand her in a way that others, even her family, had not. Perhaps it was because they'd each experienced a difficult childhood. Perhaps it was something else, something more personal and compelling, but she'd never find out what if she kept provoking him. She sighed, then concentrated on the scenery around her.

After they'd ridden on for a time, she removed her camera from one of the saddlebags and took some photographs for her book. All the while, she paid careful attention, mentally making notes. She'd write them down later, when they dismounted. The temperature escalated as the sun rose higher and higher. She was sweating, her hair felt itchy against her neck, and she wanted a drink. She put her camera away, then took a swig from her canteen. It was a relief when Adam, still riding ahead, pulled off the trail and made for a rocky outcropping.

She followed him into the shade, pushing her hat onto her back and wiping her forehead. It had to be close to a hundred and twenty Fahrenheit, she guessed. Adam dismounted, so Sierra did the same.

"Where should I tie the horse?" she asked, unable to find an anchor for the reins. At home there was always a convenient tree around. All she could see here were rocks, shrubs and the occasional cactus. "Or should we use the pickets?"

"Don't bother." Adam reached for his canteen. "They'll stay in the shade. If they do go anywhere, it'll only be to graze."

"They won't run away?" Sierra was amazed. "My horses back home would be off like a shot if they weren't tied."

"These horses won't, not in this heat. Have a drink, and find a safe spot to sit. You know what places to avoid, don't you? We have diamondback and side-winder rattlesnakes around here."

Sierra nodded. "I know what to look for. We have timber rattlers back home."

"Snakes aren't all you need to worry about," Adam warned. He capped his canteen, then started walking, stopping at the smaller rocks and dislodging them with the toe of his boot.

"What are you looking for?" Sierra asked. "A rogue lizard?"

A cocked eyebrow showed he didn't appreciate her humor.

"Ah," he said with satisfaction. "Here we go. Come and look at this."

Sierra immediately recognized the hard-shelled creature with the pointed threatening tail. "Is that a scorpion? I've never seen one in the wild before."

"Yes." Adam pushed the scorpion back under the rock with his boot.

"You aren't going to kill it?"

"No." Adam gave her a sharp look. "You object?"

"Hardly. If you think I'm going to get a case of hysterics over a few creepy-crawlies, you're sadly mistaken."

"In this case, there'd be no reason to. Scorpions don't deliberately harass humans," Adam said. "They like to hide and await their prey. Besides, there's plenty more where that one came from."

"Well, I'll keep an eye out for them."

"Make sure you do. We have about forty species in this area. Most of the bites aren't fatal to adults, just extremely painful. Like with snakes, the biggest danger is to small children and family pets."

Sierra nodded. She knew that small bodies couldn't handle the shock of the poison as well as larger ones. But forty species? She hadn't known that.

"I'll have to put that in my notes. Forty, you said?"

Adam frowned. "You don't seem very worried."

"Worried? No. But I am impressed. This is the kind of detail I need. What else can you tell me about them?"

Sierra caught the glint of approval in his eyes.

"A rule of thumb is that the lighter and larger the scorpion, the less poisonous it is. The darker the color and the smaller the size, the more dangerous. A tiny black one can kill, a bigger red one makes you very sick, and the yellow ones—they're four to six inches long and the biggest—are the least dangerous."

"I see." Sierra retrieved her camera from the saddlebag, overturned the scorpion's rock again, and took a few photos of the black scorpion as it scurried for shelter.

"Aren't you even a bit nervous?" Adam asked curiously.

Sierra finished with her photos and put the cap back on the lens. "Afraid of something I could crush with my boot heel?" She shook her head. "Don't make me laugh. Have you ever seen what a hungry Colorado grizzly can do to a steer? Or to a horse and rider?"

"No, I haven't."

"I have." Sierra trembled at the memory. "It took four shots to bring one of those bears down. My brother needed over a hundred stitches. The horse died. So don't think I'll keel over when I see a scorpion. I've seen much worse."

Adam shook his head. "Your brother's lucky he had a gun and survived the attack. He must have nerves of steel."

"My brother didn't kill that bear." Sierra's movements were jerky and stiff as she returned the camera to the saddlebag. "I did. I was twelve at the time." She reminded herself that those days were over. Her life didn't belong to the ranch anymore.

Adam watched her fuss with the saddlebags on the dozing paint, a strange expression in his eyes. "Sierra . . ."

Sierra faced him. "What?" Her response came out more sharply than she'd intended.

Adam abruptly turned back to his horse and caught the hanging reins. "The horses have rested enough. Let's go."

They rode abreast again, the sun hot on their backs. From time to time Adam pointed out particular species of cactus or birds for her, willingly stopping so Sierra could photograph them. Hawks and owls were numerous, but she was surprised to see hummingbirds flitting from cactus blossom to cactus blossom. Their dainty beauty seemed out of place in the desert.

From time to time she turned around in her saddle to study the area they had just traveled. It was easy to get lost on a return trip if you didn't, even with a guide or a well-marked trail. Her father had taught her to be prepared, and she studied the landmarks behind her on a regular basis.

Adam watched her as she swiveled back around in her seat.

"You really do know your way around the outdoors," he said approvingly. "My usual customers are hot, cranky, saddle-sore and feeling hopelessly lost by now."

"Compared to ranch life, this is a walk in the park," Sierra said, meaning every word. "Although I am hot," she admitted.

"You're doing all right in the heat so far. If all my clients were like you, I'd rest easier. You didn't even leave your tent once last night at Weldon's."

"I didn't want Sin to mistake me for a coyote stalking the chickens. You checked on me?" Sierra asked with surprise and undeniable pleasure.

"More than once. I wanted to make sure you were all right."

"You didn't stay up on my account, did you?" Sierra asked.

"I did practice a few new songs I learned on the flute," he replied, skillfully avoiding the question. "I'm assuming you slept well."

"I was fine. The sand was comfortable. Besides that, I'm no greenhorn. I've camped out a lot, in all weather, tending stock."

"You didn't like cattle ranching, did you?"

Sierra gave him a rueful smile. "It shows, huh? I left the ranch when I was eighteen and never looked back. Oh, I go home for the occasional holiday, and the weddings. All my brothers are older than I am, so one by one they're finding themselves brides as cattle-crazy as they are. I try not to stay too long. I never liked making friends with the new calves, then putting them on the train for the slaughterhouse. That was even worse than the gelding and branding. Can you imagine how traumatic it is to a child?" Sierra forced herself to remain calm, missing Adam's look of sympathy.

"You never got used to it?"

"No. Most of my brothers did, in varying degrees. So did their wives. But I was the oddball. As bad as it sounds, I don't miss my home a bit."

"I used to pray every night that I'd get a family of my very own," Adam said unexpectedly. "I don't think you should be so harsh on yours."

"Don't misunderstand me—they're good people," Sierra said quickly. "It's just that there was so much work to be done there wasn't time for..." Companionship? Affection? Love? "...anything else. I'm free of all that now. The choices I make in my life aren't dictated by a herd of cattle. I really hated them at times."

"Did you hate the cattle, or did you hate the fact that your family was so preoccupied with them?" Adam asked.

Sierra was stunned at his question, and a bit shaken by his insight. She didn't respond right away. "I don't hate either one now," she finally said. "But I spent my whole life competing with a bunch of beef for attention. Unfortunately I couldn't have one without the other, so after a while I decided to do without both. It was easier." And a lot less painful.

Adam's disapproval was plain. "I can't agree with your decision. Your parents had to earn a living somehow, and you're punishing them because they chose to ranch. Not only is it childish and unfair to them, but it's an awfully lonely way of life for you."

Sierra's eyes narrowed at his censure. She thought of all the times she'd been ignored as a child, all the times she'd been desperate for company, for affection. Her parents had always seemed more concerned about their cattle than their children—especially her. It hurt then, and it still hurt now. But that wasn't any of Adam's business.

"That sounds strange," she said, "coming from someone who spends his life in the middle of nowhere. At least I have lots of contact with people interested in history, professional people I respect. Who do *you* have, except strangers who pay you to guide them?"

"I have my Indian friends, who share their music with me. I have Weldon, and a few other people who live in the desert like I do. And I have the sisters at the orphanage. I keep in touch with them and a few of the kids I grew up with. They're the closest thing I've got to family."

"That's well and good, but trust me, the rest of the world doesn't create half the problems that family does."

"You've got it wrong," he said quietly. "The people who lived at the orphanage and my friends in the desert were always there for me. They still are. Family and friends—they're what you count on. Not the rest of the world."

The loyalty in his voice when he spoke of his friends affected Sierra more than she cared to admit. She hoped he would find the real family he wanted, but as for her, family was something to love from a distance.

"Maybe we should just agree to disagree, and drop this," Sierra said, but Adam wouldn't take her suggestion.

"I can't believe you plan to adopt. You're going to deprive that child of grandparents, uncles, aunts, and worst of all, a father. If you're lonely, it's your own choosing. It sounds as if you've decided to become a mother simply to fill a hole in your life—a hole that *you've* created.''

Sierra's jaw dropped in shock and she felt herself go rigid with anger. It was a moment before she could speak.

"How dare you? I'll make an excellent mother! I know everything a mother should do. I'll let my child help me bake cookies instead of helping with the branding. I'll teach my child how to finger paint instead of how to use a rifle to protect the family cattle. And on snowy winter mornings, I'll make my child hot chocolate and read him stories. I won't make him get on a horse and check on a herd ten miles out. I'll be a good mother because I have a lot of love to give!''

"I didn't mean you'd be an unfit parent," Adam interrupted, but a distressed Sierra couldn't stop the rush of words.

"My child will have everything I never did. He or she will want for nothing. As soon as I finish the work for this book, I'll have a steady income. My reputation will be made and I'll get that staff job! All I have to do is find the Lost Dutchman and—''

Sierra stopped abruptly when she saw Adam's face. With horror, she realized her mistake.

"So—" his eyes blazed "—you did lie. You're a treasure hunter, after all.''

CHAPTER FOUR

SIERRA FROZE in her saddle, her hands motionless on the reins. Despite her best intentions, she'd revealed what she'd intended to hide.

Adam leaned over in his saddle, grabbed her reins and stopped her horse.

"Get down," he ordered in a voice that stung like whiplash. But Sierra had already regained her senses.

"I won't." He was so angry she feared he might leave her in the middle of the desert. "You have no right to judge my private affairs."

"You lied to me, lady. You smiled that pretty little smile and lied through your teeth." Adam was furious, and he held the paint's reins with a clenched fist.

"I'm sorry. But I told the truth about who I am and what I do!"

"You hired me under false pretenses." The horses shifted nervously at his raised voice. "I should have known better. You're just another crazy treasure hunter looking for fame and fortune."

Sierra refused to be intimidated. "I'll admit I didn't tell you everything and I'm ashamed I lied. But I won't admit to being crazy, or a gold digger, either. I'm a legitimate researcher. I have a perfect right to try and make a name for myself."

"By looking for a legendary mine? You might as well waste your time searching for the pot of gold at the end of the rainbow! One is as mythical as the other. Why didn't you tell me the truth?"

"If I had, would you have listened to my reasons for wanting to find the mine? Would you have taken me on as a client?" Sierra demanded.

Adam swore a distinctly negative answer.

"That's what I thought. And that's why I kept quiet. I have to scout the Superstitions, anyway, for the book I'm doing with Tony. You get your commission and I finish my job. So what if I also indulge my dreams? It doesn't hurt anyone."

Adam glared at her, his eyes accusing. "People who live in fantasyland end up in psychiatric wards. I refuse to be a part of your delusions."

"This isn't a delusion!" Sierra shouted. Then she sighed. "Look, I don't care about finding the mine for supposed treasure. I want to find the mine so I can lay claim to a historical find! If I do, I'm virtually guaranteed a staff position with *Southwest History*. And jobs like that are few and far between. You see," she explained, "the publisher is an Arizona native, and he knows about this book. He told me he's even tried to find the Dutchman himself! He's made me a tentative offer, depending on the success of the book. So I want it to be more than just another rehashing of old facts. If I could find the Lost Dutchman, this book would be something special—it'd be a best-seller! Followed by interviews, articles, maybe a documentary. My reputation would be secure and I'd definitely get that staff job!"

"The business about your reputation I can understand, but a job at *Southwest History?* What in the world does that have to do with anything?" Adam asked, incredulous.

"The adoption agency won't let me adopt as long as I'm free-lance. Don't you see? With a staff position I'd have a regular well-paying job. Then I'd have my child."

"I can't believe what I'm hearing!"

"Adam, please! You've got to help me find the Dutchman," Sierra said desperately. "I need that job. I've spent every cent I had, including my book advance, on lawyers and pre-adoption fees."

"You're basing your whole future as a prospective parent on finding a legend? Good Lord, Sierra, you're dreaming the impossible!"

"At least I dare to dream! That seems to be a lot more than you do!" Sierra countered.

Adam recoiled as if he'd been struck. He dropped the paint's reins and Sierra gathered them tightly in her fingers again.

"Lady, you dream all you want," he said in a harsh voice. "But count me out." He whirled his horse around and slapped the reins against the Appaloosa's flanks. Sierra saw horse and rider retreat down the trail, leaving her alone with the desert.

She drew in a deep breath and found that she was trembling. What was it between the two of them that had led to this? She was positive Adam didn't tell every client about his orphaned childhood. And she'd told a perfect stranger things about her family she'd never revealed before.

She'd hurt him with that stinging remark, and she wished to heaven she'd never lied to him about her motives. If being honest from the beginning could have prevented that shocked look on Adam's face, she'd do it all over in an instant. She hated losing his respect even more than she hated being branded a liar.

Who was right? She or Adam? They'd both grown up with harsh realities. But he didn't believe in anything except those realities, while she'd decided to create something better. She thought of Adam, alone in the desert, occasionally working as guide. Maybe she *was* crazy to reach for the moon, but she preferred that to his stoic resignation any day.

A lone golden eagle circled above, its harsh cry bringing her back to the reality of the desert. Now what?

Sierra considered her options. She couldn't go any farther, not without a map. Adam had those. Although she could probably find her way out of the mountains, there was no one waiting for her with a truck and a horse trailer. Even if she rode to the Peralta trailhead and called Weldon from the ranger's office, he might not be home. And if he wasn't, she couldn't very well ride her horse down the highway all those miles to his place. For that matter, neither could Adam. Which meant he'd be stranded, too.

Sierra felt suddenly confident that he'd come back for her when he'd cooled off. He'd been too concerned for her safety all this time just to abandon her.

She decided her wisest course of action was to find a place in the shade to sit and wait. It was past noon. She wasn't hungry, but she could relax, update her notes and let the horse graze. She decided not to turn Spot loose; despite what Adam had said, she preferred not to risk having the horse run away. Best not to take chances. She unpacked the picket line and anchored it securely to horse and ground. If Adam wasn't back in a couple of hours, she'd rethink her situation.

Sierra watched the eagle circle lazily and wondered what desert creature would become its prey. Perhaps a lizard sunning itself, or a desert jack rabbit, its large heat-dispersing ears hard to hide in the sparse scrub. Life was a cruel teacher, she thought.

She closed her eyes against the sun, which still bounced and glared off the rocks, despite her position in the shade. She thought about Adam Copeland and his self-imposed solitude. It had given him a strength she envied and a simplicity of purpose she couldn't envision for herself. Then she thought of her own years of loneliness, surrounded by a large family. The kind of family Adam seemed to think he wanted. . . .

She must have dozed off, because a shadow crossed her face, waking her. At first she thought she was at the ranch.

"Is it my turn to check the stock, Dad?" she asked in a voice thick with sleep.

"It's Adam, Sierra, not your father."

"Adam?" Sierra rubbed her eyes. "Oh. I thought I was back home." She flexed her shoulders, sore from where she'd leaned against a boulder. "Even the rocks feel the same."

"Are you all right?"

She nodded. "It was just the heat. It made me drowsy. What about you? I was worried."

An unidentified expression flickered in his eyes. "It's been a long time since anyone worried about me." He continued to stand above her.

"I did worry, Adam."

"Well, it's time to start worrying about yourself. The whole canyon behind us is filled with dust devils."

"Oh, is *that* all?"

"Get on your horse, Sierra. Arizona dust devils can end up as full-blown sandstorms with eighty-mile-an-hour winds. Come on. It may be nothing, but I want us to find shelter just in case.''

Spurred on by the urgency in Adam's voice, Sierra immediately did as he said.

''There's an overhang up ahead. It's small, but we can get the horses underneath it,'' Adam said from astride the stallion. He kicked the animal into a canter, despite the heat.

She kept pace on the paint and soon saw the overhang to her left. The shaded area underneath was still quite open and exposed to the elements, but compared to the rest of the area, it provided some protection. With the horses parallel to the wall, they were sheltered from any rocks or debris falling directly overhead.

Adam dismounted and led Lightning Bolt to the narrow ledge. The ground was littered with rocks, and both horses and humans had to pick their way carefully.

''Now what?'' Sierra asked when they stood beneath the ledge.

''Now we wait.'' Adam frowned as he looked up the canyon, but Sierra saw nothing alarming. ''Make sure you hold on tightly to Spot's reins. The horses' instinct will be to outrun the storm, but they'll break a leg in this part of the canyon.''

Sierra nodded. She looped the reins tightly around one hand, then pulled her bandanna over her mouth and nose.

''Shouldn't we get out some blankets?'' she asked.

''I just have the summer-weight sleeping bags,'' Adam replied through his own blue bandanna. ''Besides, we can't watch the horses with blankets over our heads.''

Spot's tail twitched jerkily, and his nostrils flared in a snort. Adam's horse was rapidly shifting his weight from one side to the other, a sure sign of anxiety. Sierra began to feel some of their nervousness.

"Here they come," Adam said.

A whirling spout of dirt and wind came rushing down the canyon. It was only a few feet high, and Sierra breathed a sigh of relief—until she saw the one that followed. This one was perhaps six feet high and much more violent than the first. Broken pieces of vegetation swirled in among the dust.

The two dust devils danced a random pattern backward, forward and sideways. Then from the canyon came a smaller spout, then a tiny one and finally a massive one, until there were five. Each dust devil made a different whooshing sound, depending on its size, and Sierra watched with fascination as they all careened off the rocks and walls of the canyon. So far, none of them came anywhere near the ledge.

The horses skittered nervously, but the wind drowned out the sound of their iron shoes clanging on rocky ground. Sierra looked at Adam. His forehead was beaded with sweat from the stifling airless heat. Hers was, too, she realized. Their eyes met, and Adam gave her a reassuring nod.

Sierra turned back to watch the dust devils. Suddenly one of them slammed into another, and the two grew into one large spout. As if that was the signal, the other three merged with it, and one huge funnel filled the canyon. Sierra gasped as it gained strength and size, sweeping up more dust and debris, until all at once the edges of the spout had reached them.

One of the horses screamed as howling pieces of sand were driven into its delicate velvet muzzle. Sierra held tightly to the reins, closed her eyes and pulled her hat brim low on her face. It didn't help. She felt as though she was being scoured alive by sand.

Then she felt Adam's hand on her back, shoving her hard against the belly of her horse. She started to back away, not wanting her toes near the iron-shod hooves, but Adam once more pushed her face against the horse's side, sheltering it from the howling screaming sand.

This time Sierra understood what he was silently trying to tell her and she didn't resist. She buried her face in the horse's hot dusty mane. Adam's hand remained on the back of her neck. The wind was blowing her hair toward her face, and Sierra suddenly knew he was protecting her neck against the abrasive sand at the cost of his own hand.

Her fingers left the top of her hat to push his unsheltered hand away, to urge him to protect it, but Adam refused to let her. He simply covered her entire body with his, leaning his chest into her back and placing his arms tightly around her waist. His body took the brunt of the sand's punishment. Sierra was safely wedged between Adam and the horse.

She felt tears in her eyes, tears that weren't caused by the stinging sand. For what seemed like the first time in her life, she hadn't been left alone to take care of herself. She reached behind her to the back of Adam's neck and let her hand do for him what his had done for her. It was all she could do to shield him, and she fiercely wished it could be more.

Then, with a suddenness that surprised her, the giant dust devil was gone. The wind disappeared, the sand and debris fell to the ground, and the hazy cloud of dust in the desert air lingered a moment, then slowly drifted away.

Adam stepped back from her. Sierra turned around and looked at his face. There was sand in his hair, and she couldn't resist the urge to gently brush it away. Adam blinked at the contact, but he allowed her the intimacy. They both unfurled the reins, which had cut into their hands, and let them drop.

"I guess the storm's gone," she said, removing his bandanna and shaking it out. She gently wiped the sand from Adam's cheeks. "There's sand in your eyelashes. Would you...would you like me to wet the bandanna and clean them?"

"No." Adam seemed as disturbed by their new closeness as she was. "I'll do it. You look after yourself."

Sierra nodded, her hand automatically going up to smooth back her tangled hair. But she wasn't thinking about how untidy she must look. She could only think of him.

"Are you all right?" they both asked at the same time.

That broke the spell. They smiled awkwardly at each other, then Sierra shook out her own bandanna and wet it with water from the canteen.

"I'm in one piece, thanks to you. Is your hand okay?"

"I have a working man's hands," Adam replied. "It's just fine."

"I'm glad." Sierra cleaned her face and rewet the bandanna. "You'll still be able to play your flute." She began the delicate job of cleaning sand from the paint's eyes, while Adam ministered to his stallion. "Maybe someday you'll play some of your songs for me?"

Sierra didn't see Adam's startled expression, then his smile. "Maybe."

"As long as it isn't an ode to a sandstorm," she said lightly, finishing with Spot's eyes and starting on his nostrils.

Adam was amused. "Sierra, that was no storm. Those were just plain old dust devils."

"That was a storm," she stubbornly insisted.

"No." Adam chuckled. "Real storms last much longer, and they're much more violent."

"That wasn't violent?" Sierra stuffed the soiled bandanna in the saddlebag. "Let me show you something." She sat down on the nearest large rock and pulled off her boot. "Look at this." She held the boot upside down, pouring out a pile of sand.

"That was a storm," she announced again.

"That was a dust devil. Now a sandstorm—" Adam finished with his horse and proceeded to empty his boots "—a *real* sandstorm would have torn your boots right off your feet. You've seen Weldon's truck?"

"The one with the bad paint job?"

"Yes. He got caught in a sandstorm with it soon after he bought it—brand-new, I might add. By the time the storm was over, the winds and the sand had scoured the paint right off."

"Y-you're joking."

"No. The colored finish was completely gone, down to the bare metal. And you know car insurance doesn't cover 'acts of God' unless you pay extra."

"And Weldon hadn't?"

"No. He was fit to be tied. Couldn't believe his bad luck. Hence his present bad paint job."

Sierra bit her lip. Just thinking about Adam in such a ferocious storm was very unsettling.

"Now *that,* Sierra, was a sandstorm."

Sierra watched as Adam pulled on his boots and stood up again. She emptied her remaining boot, then slid her feet back in.

She lifted her hands to his for help in getting up. It was an automatic gesture, one she'd made to her brothers during countless trail rides and camping trips. After a heartbeat's pause, Adam took her hands in his and drew her to her feet. But where her brothers would have let go the instant she was standing, Adam continued to hold her.

Sierra remembered the feel of his body against hers and didn't pull away. Something seemed to flow between them—respect, sympathy and a strange sweet excitement.

"Thank you for looking after me," she said. "And I want to apologize. I shouldn't have lied to you about wanting to search for the Dutchman. Will you still guide me?"

The reference to the mine brought a frown to Adam's face. He released her, but not before his thumb traced one last trail on her palm.

"I'll still guide you," he said, but seeing Sierra's joy, added, "against my better judgment."

"Thank you." Relief flooded through her. She could still complete her plans, still make a name for herself as a historian of the Southwest. Most important, she could still attain the job and the income necessary to qualify for adoption.

"In fact, not only will I guide you, but I intend to help you look for the mine."

Sierra couldn't believe her good fortune, and her eyes opened wide with surprise. "You will?"

"Yes."

"You . . . you aren't angry?"

"I was very angry, but that was before."

Before what? Before the storm? Sierra wondered.

"I still don't agree with you," he went on. "But I have to earn a living, too."

Sierra felt a surge of disappointment at his practical reason for continuing with their arrangement, but she was determined not to show it.

"How can I thank you properly? Would you like more money? I could clear it with Tony. You know I couldn't offer you gold," she reminded him. "If I find any, the government owns it."

Adam shook his head. "I don't want anyone's money. In fact, I want to do this for nothing." He reached inside his buttoned shirt pocket and withdrew the check she had given him. "Here. Here's your deposit back."

"I can't take this! Supplies cost, and renting the horse does, too!"

"I don't want it." He ripped it in half, and shoved the pieces in her breast pocket before Sierra could push his fingers away.

"Then what *do* you want?" she asked in confusion. "A percentage of the royalties? Tony would have to agree..." She frowned. "What if I split the payment for anything else I publish about the Dutchman's discovery? And what if I include a written mention that you were my guide?"

"Nothing." Adam waved the offers away with a flick of his hand. "I told you, I don't want any money, or a business plug, either. I don't want to advertise the fact that I'm guiding a wild-goose chase."

"You don't believe I'll succeed, but you'll still help me try to find the Lost Dutchman?" Sierra planted her hands on her hips.

"Yes. I'll do everything I can. I'll check out every hunch you have, every whim."

"This sounds too good to be true. There *has* to be a catch," she said suspiciously. Nothing in life came without a sacrifice. The ranch had taught her that.

"I wouldn't call it a catch. A condition, perhaps."

"I thought so." Sierra took in a deep breath, then exhaled. "All right, let's hear it."

"If I can accommodate you against my better judgment, then you can do the same for me. I want you to consider giving up your plans to adopt a child."

"That's insane! I can't believe you'd say that!"

Adam crossed his arms over his chest. "I think it's insane to deny a child the benefits of two parents. You can't possibly realize the damage you could do."

"It's none of your business! Look, I'm sorry you were raised in an orphanage, and I'm sorry you were never adopted. But I can't allow you to influence me. I want to have a child, and I'd be a good mother."

"You'd be a better one if that child had a father, too!"

"Right now, that's out of the question."

"I don't understand your big rush to adopt," Adam told her. "You're young, Sierra. And you're an intelligent attractive woman. There's no reason you shouldn't marry someday and have your own children." Adam studied her carefully. "Or is there?"

Sierra immediately shied away from his question. "For someone who likes to keep to himself, you're awfully interested in my personal life. I'd like to know why."

"Obviously this is a sensitive subject with you," Adam said quietly.

Yes, it *was* sensitive. Painfully so. She was a sterile woman whose fiancé hadn't wanted her because of it. But she wasn't about to share that pain with Adam.

"You still haven't answered my question," she retorted. "Why are you so concerned?"

Much to her surprise and relief, Adam dropped his questions and answered hers instead. "Because this is important to me, too. For personal reasons. I told you about my failed adoption attempt."

"Go on."

"What I didn't tell you was that she was a writer. Like you."

"A writer?" Sierra repeated, surprised.

"Yes, like you. Sit down, Sierra."

The two of them shared space on one of the bigger rocks. Adam took off his hat and worked it around and around.

"Her name was Melanie. She was an American, from Arizona, and she wrote poetry. She'd just sold her first book. Her finances seemed sound."

"That's why she was granted custody of you, even though she wasn't a Mexican national?"

"Melanie's nationality had nothing to do with it. Mexico allowed U.S. citizens to adopt Mexican children back then, and still does. The fact that she was Catholic and seemed reasonably well off were the main factors. Unfortunately, there was a long dry spell between the first book and the second, which is why I ended up back in the orphanage. Don't you see, Sierra? If she'd had a husband, he could have helped support us during that lean period. But there was no one else, no husband, no family. So it was back to the orphanage for me, even though neither of us wanted it.''

Sierra was aghast. ''Adam, I'm so sorry. I'm sure she only did what she thought best. I'm sure she was trying to put your welfare first.''

''I know she was. She even tried to readopt me when she had money again.''

''Melanie came back for you?''

Adam nodded. The hat in his hands continued to make its circles.

''Adam, she must have loved you.''

A vein in Adam's temple throbbed. ''I came to that conclusion, too, but not soon enough. I kept refusing to see her, and the time between her attempted visits grew longer and longer. Finally she stopped coming to the orphanage altogether. I told myself that was what I wanted, but . . . It wasn't until I left the university that I finally tried to contact her.''

''Did you find her?''

''I found her headstone.'' Adam's voice was harsh. ''She'd been killed in a car accident. She'd never married, never tried to adopt another child. All I have left of Melanie is the two books of poetry she wrote, and an old photograph. And a lot of guilt.''

Sierra touched his shoulder. ''Adam, you were only a child. You can't blame yourself. Remember what you said to me? That sometimes circumstances dictate actions? This is one of those awful, sad times.''

Adam shook off her hand by rising to his feet.

''I'm only telling you this so you can see what a big mistake you're making. And that's why I'll still guide you. I'll even help you find the Lost Dutchman, lost cause though it is. All I ask is that you allow me to try and change your mind about single-parent adoption. I don't want history to repeat itself at another orphan's expense. If you're so sure of yourself, anything I say couldn't hurt, right?''

Sierra's heart ached at his pain. She knew how a difficult childhood could haunt one's adult life. Although she resented Adam's interference, how could she fault him for allowing his own childhood to influence his actions? That was no more than she was doing.

Adam saw her dilemma and pressed his advantage. "All I'm asking is your permission to be more than just an impersonal guide on this trip. I want a fair hearing, with conversation as intimate as it takes to get my point across.''

"Intimate?'' That was a strange thing for him to say. The world unsettled her. "We hardly know each other.''

"We've got a whole week to ourselves.''

Sierra bit her lower lip and considered. "I don't have to make any ridiculous promises? Don't forget I'm already on the waiting list for a child.''

"No. All I want is you to listen to me with an open mind.''

That didn't sound so bad. Still, Sierra hesitated.

"I'm the only guide around,'' Adam reminded her. "You have no where else to turn.''

Her eyes met his. "Then heaven help us both.''

AFTER A QUICK LUNCH, which neither of them wanted, they mounted up again. Once they were back on the trail, Adam proved true to his word.

"What would you like to know about the Lost Dutchman?'' he asked.

Sierra shrugged. She wasn't really in the mood to talk and found it strangely difficult to concentrate on the mine.

Adam finally broke the uncomfortable silence that had fallen between them. "No questions? Remember, we have a deal."

"I did do my research," Sierra replied tartly. "Jacob Waltz was born in Germany—not in Holland. He was a rancher, farmer, prospector and miner, depending on what work was available. He made some documented silver and gold strikes, but his wealthy periods alternated with very poor ones. In 1891 the Salt River flooded and washed away his house and everything in it. He caught pneumonia and was taken into the home of a friend, Julia Thomas. He died there, in his late sixties or early seventies. His exact date of birth is unknown."

"You've done your homework. But isn't there anything you want to ask?"

Sierra gave him a sidelong glance. Adam's face was hidden in the shadow of his broad hat brim. She turned her own eyes back to the trail. "I don't have any more questions. I'd rather just ride and look at the scenery right now."

That was the truth. For the first time since she'd met Adam, she felt uncomfortable in his presence. Earlier, there had been an unspoken camaraderie between them. Now, all she could think about was the strength of his strong body pressed against hers. The gentleness of his palm on her neck. And how, despite her dishonesty, he'd come back to warn her about the dust devils. But Adam wouldn't accept her silence. He turned toward her, and Sierra could feel his gaze. Finally she shifted in her saddle, acknowledging him.

"What did you and your brothers talk about when you rode together?" he asked curiously.

"My brothers?" Sierra was surprised at the question. "They never simply talked. They were always arguing about who could handle the worst horse, who could rope the quickest steer, who could do the most work."

"You didn't have a very big part in those conversations, then?"

"On the contrary. As the only woman—and, in their opinion, out of the running—I was often consulted during the disputes. I tried to be as fair as possible, but no matter what I decided, I could never make everyone happy. My opinion was always considered biased by four out of the five. Those rides could get pretty noisy, what with all the yelling." She smiled at the memory. "I swear our horses ended up with hearing loss."

"So who *was* the best cowhand?"

Sierra thought about that. "It's hard to say. Paul was the oldest. He was by far the hardest worker, but he wasn't much fun. He didn't talk, didn't smile, just did the job. Pairing up with him was a mixed blessing. We always finished our chores first, but it never seemed that way. He could be awfully dull company."

"Who was next?"

"That would be Eric. He's a real character." Sierra grinned. "Eric loves to sleep and hates to work. But he has the greatest sense of humor. Brother or not, he's the funniest guy I've ever known. I'd end up doing my work and most of his, but I'd always come home with a stitch in my side from laughing. That was okay in the summer, but in the winter he was a man to avoid. I didn't want to be out in the cold any longer than I had to."

Adam listened avidly. It seemed to Sierra that he was hungry to see how an actual family lived.

"I see your point. Who came next?"

"Drew and Scott, the twins. Together, they could move mountains. But they hated being separated, and never worked well with anyone else. They even ended up marrying two sisters who had the same kind of relationship. I never knew the twins as well as I knew my other brothers. They tended to shut the rest of us out."

"That's too bad."

"Yes. But that's the way they are."

"And the last brother?"

"That's Jonathan. He's the youngest of the men. I was born shortly after him, so we were pretty close. In fact, he's the only one of the boys who writes to me on a regular basis."

"What kind of a person is he?"

Sierra adjusted her sunglasses before answering. "Well, he's hard to describe. Jon can work as hard as Paul on the one hand and be as charming as Eric on the other, yet he's completely different from both. He used to really spoil me during chores."

"How?"

"Jon was stubborn. When we were teamed up, he insisted on doing most of the dirty work. He'd make me take the lighter stuff, even though he didn't like cattle much more than I did. I'll never forget that," Sierra said fervently. "What's more, he was the only one who stuck up for me when I decided to stop eating red meat."

"You're a vegetarian?"

"Yes. It drove Dad crazy. He said I was a disgrace to the ranch."

Adam frowned. "I find that hard to believe. No one could fault you, considering your ranch chores."

"You're wrong. Dad wouldn't even allow me to eat with the rest of the family until I gave up what he called my 'ridiculous notions.' I wouldn't change my mind, and neither would he. I was sent to the kitchen to eat alone. Jon decided to join me, although he wasn't a vegetarian."

"Did your father ever change his mind?"

"Eventually, after a few weeks. It finally took Mom to convince Dad to give in. I'll never forget how Jon supported me. My other brothers didn't."

Sierra swallowed hard. She'd never admit it, but she missed her youngest brother, perhaps more than she'd ever expected.

"We both hated ranch life. The two of us used to plot our escape. We'd dream about finding gold on the ranch and fantasize about how we'd escape with it. Old legends always appealed to him. In fact, we knew about the Lost Dutchman mine as kids. I never dreamed I'd actually end up looking for it. It's too bad Jon couldn't be here with us. He'd love this. It'd be like a childhood dream come true."

"What's he doing now?"

"Jon's the only one of my brothers who's unmarried. He's on the rodeo circuit now. Mom says she sees less and less of him. If any of them ever leaves ranch life, it'll be Jon."

"He sounds like a good man to have as a friend. And your other brothers sound all right, too. You may have had strict parents, but it doesn't sound like such a bad family," Adam observed.

"It wasn't, I guess, but it would have been so much better if we'd had time for each other." Sierra shrugged. "But what about you? Tell me about your childhood."

"I thought you wanted to hear about the Lost Dutchman."

"Perhaps I'm more interested in hearing about you," she said boldly.

Adam threw her a sharp look, but Sierra was certain she saw a flash of pleasure in his expression.

"What did you do for fun as a child?" she prompted. "I don't imagine you spent your time like I did." It seemed the more she knew about him, the more she wanted to know.

"No." After a moment he elaborated. "There were no wide open spaces for us. We spent our days within the confines of the orphanage. The older boys watched the younger boys, just as the older girls watched the younger ones. You grew up tending cattle. Well, I grew up tending children, all ages, all shapes, all sizes." Adam's face softened.

"I used to go crazy sometimes, trying to amuse those kids. But the nuns were shorthanded. They had all they could do to take care of the babies and teach in the classrooms. So there I was, with a passel of children, and just a child myself. When I was at my wit's end, I used to sing them silly songs."

"Silly songs?" Sierra couldn't quite see the serious man before her singing lighthearted ditties.

Adam nodded. "I played the organ in our local church. All of us were taught to sing hymns in Spanish, English and sometimes Latin during Mass. I loved music, and when the girl who originally played the organ was adopted, I took her place." He grinned. "Only sometimes the songs I taught them weren't in the hymnals."

"I imagine young children could find those hymns pretty boring after a while."

"They certainly did. When we were supposed to be rehearsing for the choir, we'd sometimes sing rounds of 'Three Blind Mice' and 'Row, Row, Row Your Boat,' and Mexican songs you wouldn't be familiar with. The younger children considered them much more fun than hymns."

"Did you sing in the choir, too?"

"Before I became the organist, I did. I was a better organist than a vocalist, though, because my voice tended to crack in my teen years. I eventually ended up playing the music for all the Masses and weddings. The nuns used to compliment me. They said I hadn't been adopted because the angels wanted to keep such a good organist in the church."

Adam's gaze grew distant, and Sierra wished she dared stretch her hand the short distance between them.

"What a lovely thing to say to a child."

"Yes, it was. Anyway, I continued with my music. The orphanage sent me to university, where I studied voice and organ. I didn't go back after I graduated, because they already had a new organist. I tried city life, gave it up and stumbled into this. End of story."

Sierra thought privately that there were a lot of gaps in his story, gaps she wanted him to fill. Such as, did he ever date? Couldn't he find the right woman out of all those he must have met at university and in his music career? Then she wondered if she should forget such personal questions, at least for now. She should be concentrating on finding the Lost Dutchman mine, she told herself.

Sierra checked the position of the sun in the sky. It was late afternoon, and starting to cool down. They'd be stopping soon. She vowed to find out more about Adam's life then.

"All right," she said abruptly. "You want to talk about the mine, let's talk about the mine." She drew a resolute breath. "According to what I've unearthed in my research, there are three theories about the origins of the Dutchman legend."

"Only three?" Adam's voice bordered on disbelief. "There's a lot more than that."

"I don't count the more bizarre theories. We don't deal in UFOs or ghostly apparitions in our book."

"Good idea. Which theories did you keep?"

"Tony likes the Aztec treasure theory. Supposedly Montezuma hid most of the Aztec gold in the Superstitions to keep it safe from the Spanish Conquistadors. Jacob Waltz could have found the gold instead of mining it."

"You can discard that one. Even if the Aztecs did cache their hoard, it's unlikely Jacob Waltz discovered it. The Aztecs were quite skilled in gold refinement. The majority of the old assayers' records on Jacob Waltz say he had gold ore in his possession, not refined gold."

Sierra nodded. "My research confirms that, but he also had some gold assayed that was of a highly refined quality. I checked all those old assayers' records. Still, I'll admit it's the least probable of the theories."

"Which other ones do you have?" Adam asked.

"There's the massacre gold theory."

Adam nodded. "That's my favorite."

"Why?"

"It's the most logical. The Apache Indians used the Superstitions as their stronghold. The Pima and Maricopa Indians farmed the surrounding bottomlands of the Superstitions, and everyone was involved in skirmishes with the Apaches regarding territorial rights. When gold was discovered in the mountains and miners also started invading Apache territory, this added to the bloodshed.''

''I know the Apaches used horses, not gold, as their monetary system,'' Sierra said.

''At first gold was just a useless metal to them. Then they grew to hate it for drawing unwanted people to their land. The Apaches would ambush any miners and deliberately scatter the gold on the mountain floor, hence the term 'massacre gold.' Jacob Waltz could easily have discovered a large supply of that. It's one of the better explanations for his sudden wealth, and accounts for the refined ore in his possession.''

''But not many people believe that theory.''

Adam's lips twisted unpleasantly. ''No. They're more willing to believe fairy tales than the truth.''

Sierra flushed. She couldn't tell if he was directing that particular comment at her or not, but before she managed to come up with a response, he asked, ''What was your last theory?''

''The Peralta mine.''

''That's another iffy explanation. What do you know about the Peraltas?''

''I know that this trail we're on was named after them. I also know they were a wealthy Mexican family. They could afford to pay laborers to take most of the risks with the Apaches. For three generations they mined gold in the Superstitions.''

''That's right. They mined until 1848, when the Mexican Superstitions were granted to the United States by treaty.''

''As Mexican citizens, the Peraltas couldn't claim title to the mine anymore,'' Sierra remembered. ''Supposedly they also decided they had more than enough wealth and massacred laborers, so they stopped their mining operations when the treaty became effective.''

"That much is fact,'' Adam agreed. "But nothing else about the legend is documented. The worst thing about that particular theory is the claim that old Peralta maps with the mine's location still exist. I must hear that every year from some crazy treasure hunter.''

"Couldn't there be? According to the old newspapers, Waltz met the Peraltas in Mexico,'' Sierra argued. "Apparently Don Miguel Peralta offered Waltz the mine, a map and all the gold he could find, since he no longer had title.''

"I find that a little hard to believe. It isn't in human nature to be so generous.''

"It could be true,'' Sierra insisted. "I know Waltz had a partner, a man by the name of Wiese. They set out for the Peralta mine together, and returned with gold from *somewhere*. The original Peralta mine could have been the Lost Dutchman.''

Adam wasn't convinced. "That's ridiculous. Newspapers back then printed so-called eyewitness accounts without verifying their accuracy. Wiese was killed by the Apaches, Waltz died of pneumonia, and no one knows if they found their gold in the Peralta mine or not. Even if they did, there couldn't have been much gold left. The location of the Peralta mine was no secret. Too much hired labor worked it. The mine would have been stripped clean soon after the Peraltas lost title to it, if the Peraltas hadn't stripped it already.''

"Still, that doesn't mean there isn't a legitimate mine left to be discovered. It seems a shame not to know more than hearsay and rumors about it.''

Adam's gaze was penetrating. "That's why the story of the mine is a *legend*," he emphasized. "Don't take it too seriously."

She couldn't allow his remark to remain unchallenged. "And if I do?"

"If you've done your research, you know the Lost Dutchman mine is supposed to be cursed. If you've read all those old newspapers, you're aware that most of those gold seekers paid the ultimate price for their greed."

Sierra did remember those tragic accounts. Even worse, many of the tragedies weren't so ancient, either. In fact, some were quite uncomfortably recent.

Adam studied her worried face. "So you do know," he said softly. "Those who search for the treasure usually end up dead."

Sierra felt a chill go down her spine as he added, "These mountains aren't called the Superstitions for nothing."

CHAPTER FIVE

THE SUN HADN'T SET, but it had fallen beneath the peaks and spires of the Superstitions. Orange light filtered through, giving the mountains a burnished metallic glow. In other circumstances, Sierra might have enjoyed the effect. As it was, she still felt too upset by her conversation with Adam to fully appreciate the uniqueness of the sunset.

She watched him wash his plate and silverware in the sand and repack it. She followed suit, knowing water was precious, but she also carefully wiped her dishes and utensils with a fresh bandanna.

"That isn't going to get them much cleaner," Adam told her.

Sierra didn't comment. She didn't care if he thought her fastidious.

"You've been awfully quiet since we set up camp," he observed. "Was the heat too much for you?"

"Not at all." She checked on her tent stakes one more time, worried that they might loosen in the sandy ground.

"Then what's the problem?"

Sierra straightened. "If you must know, I don't appreciate your scare tactics. But it'll take more than a few stories of cursed gold mines and bodies in the desert to change my mind."

"The number of fatalities in these mountains is no fairy tale. And I'm not talking about Apache-caused deaths of a century ago. I'm talking about present-day treasure hunters dying in these mountains. At least we assume they're dead. Sometimes they simply disappear."

"So you've said." Sierra glanced at her picketed horse before unpacking her ground cloth and sleeping bag. "And frankly, I've heard more than enough. Every rich mining area, from Leadville, Colorado, to California's Sutters Mill, has its stories of greed and death."

"So they do. But those places haven't had any prospectors die lately, have they? The Superstitions have. Just watch the news."

Sierra opened her ground cloth with a loud snap and shook it free of trail dust. "I'm not a prospector," she retorted as she entered her tent and spread it on the ground. "So I'm not going to worry."

"That's not my point."

Sierra came out to retrieve her sleeping bag. "What is, then?" she asked irritably.

"You're taking an awful lot of risks for something that probably doesn't exist."

"Maybe I am." She unfastened the bag and gave it a quick shake. "But you're guiding me. And what's more, you're doing it for nothing. You tell me who's crazier."

Sierra went back in the tent, and after a careful check for unwanted crawling guests, spread the bag atop the ground cloth. She took in a deep breath, trying to calm herself. Tomorrow they'd reach Weavers Needle. If she wanted a good night's sleep, she'd better get her thoughts back on the Dutchman and away from Adam

Copeland. Unfortunately that was proving rather difficult....

She crept out again to bring her saddle and saddlebags inside the tent, in case it rained during the night. Adam picked them up and did it for her.

"Thank you." Must the man be so considerate? She'd never be able to ignore him at this rate—especially since she suspected she didn't really want to.

"You're welcome." Adam stowed his own saddle in his tent, but left the saddlebags out. "You didn't eat much of your dinner."

"I just can't eat in this heat."

"It'll cool down now the sun's gone."

Sierra nodded. She could feel the change in the air already.

"I could fix you something later on."

"Don't worry about it. I'll eat a big breakfast in the morning. If you don't mind, I'm going to call it a night. I'll catch up on my notes, then go to sleep."

"You could keep me company," Adam said quietly.

That brought Sierra to a halt. Adam actually sounded lonely. Traveling on her own as much as she did, she understood the craving for companionship, for conversation and sharing. Suddenly she knew that he'd offered to cook her another meal not only because he was considerate, but because he wanted her to stay. "If it isn't too much bother, I could use something to snack on," she said. "A piece of fruit, perhaps."

Adam immediately rose. "I've got some apples."

"That would be nice." She leaned against a large rock, and Adam soon joined her. They sat, relaxed and silent, savoring the coolness of the night air.

"I wasn't trying to scare you away with horror stories earlier," Adam explained as Sierra ate. "But I've seen so many people hurt—and dead—out here in the desert. The thought of your being one of them..." His voice drifted off and he shook his head. "I refuse to let you become a statistic."

"I won't. And it'll take more than a few scary stories to frighten me away," Sierra said with a smile.

"I've already gathered that. You're the first tourist who hasn't screamed my ears deaf during a dust devil."

Sierra gave up pretending an interest in her apple. She tossed the remains over to Spot. The paint immediately picked up the treat with eager lips.

Sierra turned toward Adam and tried to make out his face in the dark. Very little moonlight shone through the cloudy sky.

"About that... Thank you for taking care of me during the sandstorm. I mean dust devil. It was a lot less nerve-racking with you there."

"You're welcome. But thanks aren't needed. I do the same for all my customers."

"Do you?" Sierra asked quietly. "Do you cover their necks with your own hand?"

Adam traced a path down her cheek with one finger. "Not all my customers have such soft skin. Remember Weldon's truck? I didn't want that to happen to you."

"I still want to say thanks." Sierra lifted her hand to his shoulder. His body felt warm and welcoming under her palm.

"I know you're from snow country. Why do you seem so at home in the desert?" He pulled her closer with an arm around her waist, his lips a mere fraction from hers. "Why do you seem so at home in my arms?"

Sierra's soft response, "Because I think I am," was never heard. Adam's lips covered hers in a gentle kiss, a kiss that felt honest and right, that left her straining for more. It came as a shock when Adam broke the embrace.

"Perhaps you'd better get to bed," he said. "It's late, and I shouldn't keep you up any longer."

Sierra's heart sank with disappointment. She slowly withdrew, removing her hand from his shoulder. "Thanks for the apple." This careful politeness seemed at odds with their intimacy of a moment before.

"Thank you for letting me get it. I know you didn't really want it."

Sierra blushed. "No, but I did want the company. Good night, Adam."

"Sierra... Make sure you shake out your boots when you get up in the morning," he said.

Sierra paused at the entrance to her tent, touched by his words. The fact that he knew she was a capable outdoorsperson made her cherish his concern even more. "I will. I always do, anyway. There are creepy-crawlies in Colorado, too."

"Not like ours. Besides the scorpions, we have tarantulas out here. Don't forget."

"I thought you promised no more scary stories," she reproached gently, reluctant to let the night end.

"This is the desert. A little healthy respect is never amiss."

"Adam?" She paused. "If you're going to stay up, would you play your flute for me?"

She felt his answering smile in the darkness. "A few songs, if you wish."

"I'd like that," she said.

Sierra had undressed and was crawling into her sleeping bag when the clear notes of the flute began. The unfamiliar melody was haunting and beautiful, swelling with a life of its own in the night air. Sierra suspected the song was Adam's own composition. Suddenly she heard two reed flutes. The new flute played what she recognized as traditional music, while Adam's flute skillfully wove new notes among the old.

If she wasn't afraid of breaking the spell, Sierra would have dressed and left the tent to see who had joined Adam. As it was, she could have listened all night to the music. She was sitting up in her bag, wide-eyed when one of the flutes gradually became softer and softer, then was silent. A few minutes later Adam's flute breathed its last reedy notes and was also still.

Sierra's eyes filled with tears. There had been such beauty and passion in the song that she hated to hear it end.

"Sierra, are you still awake?" Adam asked softly.

"Yes." Through the wall of her tent Sierra could see the glow of the fire go out as Adam threw sand on it. "Adam, that was beautiful. Who else was with you?"

"A friend of mine."

"One of your Indian friends?"

"Yes."

"It was—" she hesitated "—almost as if that song was written just for me."

Silence.

"Thank you, Adam."

"You're welcome. Now go to sleep. I'll see you in the morning."

Sierra smiled to herself and nestled into the sleeping bag. But it was long before morning when Sierra saw Adam again. A violent noise woke her and she opened her eyes to see flashing lights in the darkness outside. She recognized the noise as thunder and quickly dressed, then shook out her boots and pulled them on.

As she hurried out of her tent, she saw that Adam, also dressed, was watching the sky.

Far past the peaks, multiple flashes of lightning were dancing across purple clouds. Flash after flash of brightness lit up the night sky, followed by booming thunder.

Sierra gasped in amazement. It was a thunderstorm, but a thunderstorm such as she'd never seen before. The lightning traveled not only diagonally but vertically, horizontally and in circles. The flashes seemed to be playing hide-and-seek with one another in the clouds.

Adam reached for her hand and pulled her next to him. "Welcome to monsoon season."

Sierra pushed her tousled hair away from her face. The air was heavy with the smell of far-off rain. "I've never seen anything like this. The night clouds are actually bright," she said with wonder. "And that storm must be miles away."

"It is."

They both watched the lights. "How long will this last?" Sierra asked.

"An hour. Maybe two or three. Fortunately it won't reach us tonight. The last thing we need is rain in these narrow canyons."

"What about tomorrow?" Sierra asked, worried about her prospects of finding the Lost Dutchman. "Will it be safe to travel?"

"We'll have to be careful and keep a close eye on the thunderheads. They start building when the heat peaks and usually reach storm capacity by late afternoon."

Even from this distance, Sierra was awed by the power locked within those light-streaked purple clouds. "I've never seen anything like this. I always thought the desert was so peaceful."

"There's a dark side to everything, Sierra. Don't you know that?"

Sierra shivered. After a moment, she asked, "Should I check on the horses?"

"I already did. The storm's far away. They won't spook." His grip on her fingers loosened, then her hand fell away. "You can go back to bed if you want."

Sierra knew she was being dismissed. She returned to her tent, all the while wondering how much longer Adam would watch the sky with eyes as wild as the storm itself.

THE NEXT MORNING a short ride took them to the base of Weavers Needle. As they hiked to its peak, Sierra found herself humming bits of the song he had played for her the night before. The haunting melody keep replaying in her mind and interfering with her concentration. She felt sure it was a love ballad, or was that just her overactive imagination? She had to practically force herself to take notes, snap three rolls of film and familiarize herself with the area.

By lunchtime her efforts paid off. She had most of what she needed for the book. She'd fully documented the vegetation and the landscape, as well as the Needle, which did indeed look like a half-buried heart. A few more notes and photographs when they reached the old water holes would complete her work, but Adam wouldn't be taking her there for days yet.

Her next step was to do some treasure hunting. She needed to consult Adam's map; her own maps were all old, and the one she'd ordered from the Department of the Interior had been left with Tony. Her plan was to compare the new maps with those from the late nineteenth century. Naturally, none of the old maps marked the location of the Lost Dutchman. That would have been too much to hope for, Sierra thought wryly. In fact, it was the differences between the old and new maps that made the mine's detection so difficult.

"I'm through with my pictures. Ready to hike back down to the horses? We can have lunch whenever you want," she suggested.

Adam nodded and led the way. The air was hot and sticky. Sierra's shirt was soaked by the time they reached the bottom of East Boulder Canyon, the area below Weavers Needle. She unfastened her blue paisley bandanna and mopped her face.

"It feels like it's going to rain," she said, fanning herself with her hat.

Adam checked the clouds. "It will, but it won't reach us. Look at the thunderheads."

Sierra watched the thunderheads above the finger-like rock formations. The clouds were building ever higher in the northern sky, ominous and purple.

"They're too far north," Adam said.

"If it doesn't rain, how will the horses drink?"

"Since we didn't tie them, they should have watered while we were up on Weavers Needle. I found enough pockets for them this morning before we set off. They can smell water, you know. Don't worry."

"It's just so different. Back home there're always streams because of all the snow and runoff."

"We have streams, too. There's Willow Springs near First Water Trail, where Weldon will be picking us up. Canyon Lake and Salt River are north of that. We'll find other spots even closer, so don't worry. Let's eat before it gets much hotter."

Sierra took the peanut-butter-and-jelly sandwich and the raisins he passed her. They sat side by side on a flat sun-warmed rock.

"It's strange to think of lakes in the desert. And that reminds me," Sierra said. "When we're done eating, can I check your map? I have copies of some old ones, but Tony has my new one."

Adam ate some beef jerky. "My map doesn't have an X-marks-the-spot on it any more than your old ones do."

"Very funny." Sierra washed down the dry bread with a swig from her canteen. "I want to see how much the trails have changed over the years."

"Does this mean you're ready to start treasure hunting now?"

Sierra saw no point in sidestepping the issue. "Yes."

Adam continued eating. "You'll be disappointed if you intend to pinpoint the supposed location by comparing the old maps with the new ones."

"How did you know that's what I'm going to do?" Sierra asked with surprise.

"It's a logical assumption. But I really doubt you'll have much success."

"You're wrong. As a researcher, I have access to historical archives the public doesn't. I've gone through the rare documents archived at the State House, and I've narrowed the search area down considerably."

Adam gave her a look of pity mixed with exasperation. "Sierra, you can't compare old maps to new. The Superstitions are a fragile rock formation. The feldspar spires break all the time. The landscape doesn't remain the same from one year to the next."

"I know that. I've made allowances."

"Did you make allowances for the earthquake?"

Sierra felt a moment's panic. "What earthquake?"

"In the late 1800s an earthquake hit south-central Arizona. The Superstitions were right in the middle of that earthquake zone. The landscape suffered extensive damage." Adam frowned. "I thought you did your research."

"What kind of damage?" Sierra asked frantically, racking her brain for any mention of an earthquake in her reading.

"Large slabs of rock broke off from their original positions. Trenches were filled, old trails covered, new ledges exposed. The land was heavily altered. The quake made the old maps virtually useless."

"But some of my older maps must have been drawn up after the earthquake," Sierra insisted.

"It doesn't matter. The only way you could find an existing mine would be to use those old maps with the old topography. But that's obviously impossible. Don't you see? Jacob Waltz is supposed to have found the mine *before* the earthquake."

"Before? Are you sure?"

"Yes. Legend says Waltz discovered his gold in the 1870s. The earthquake was on May 3, 1887. You didn't know, did you?"

"I...no." Her confidence shaken, Sierra felt her heart grow cold. She had a reputation as a thorough researcher. How could she have made such a terrible omission? "This can't be a well-documented fact! I would've discovered it!"

"It's not commonly known," Adam agreed. "I only found out about the earthquake when I was studying the geology of the area. And even then, most of the books don't mention it, although there are a few references in the newspapers of that year. The earthquake was actually documented by a nearby army post, Fort McDowell. But it didn't cause any fatalities, which I guess is why it disappeared from the record books. Will this alter your plans? What will you do?''

Sierra hated hearing the pity in his voice. "I'll just have to... to work around it."

"What happens if you don't find the Lost Dutchman?" he pressed.

"I'll find it," she replied, but her answer lacked her usual conviction.

"For argument's sake, what if you don't? Does that mean you might not get the *Southwest History* job— you'll have to keep free-lancing?"

Sierra brushed the bread crumbs from her jeans with unsteady hands. "I suppose so. Why?"

"You couldn't adopt, could you, if you're traveling all over the country? You can't drag a child along on expeditions like this. And once the child gets older, he'll have to go to school. Then what?"

"I intend to be solidly established by then."

"That takes years and years of work." Adam's face was full of disapproval. "You told me you've been cleared for adoption already, and you're on the waiting list. If they call you tomorrow, what will you tell them?"

Sierra was still reeling from hearing about the earthquake. "I'd deal with that when it comes up," she said in a shaky voice.

"How? By finding another job that wouldn't require travel?"

She nodded, biting her lip.

"Such as?" Adam was relentless. "What else do you know how to do?"

Sierra shook her head helplessly. "I don't really know anything else, except ranching."

"Would you work a cattle ranch again so that you'd be home for your child?"

"I…" She rubbed her forehead in dismay. Could she go back to that hated way of life, even if it meant being a mother? Could she even contemplate it?

"Well, Sierra?"

"I don't know!"

Adam rose to his feet. "You'd better know before an agency places a child in your arms. And you'd better not base your hopes of adoption on finding a mythical gold mine."

Sierra also got up. "And if I do?" she challenged.

"If you do, you might end up giving that child right back again. And that's something I'd never, ever forgive."

Sierra watched him stride away to retrieve the untied horses. She sat back down on the rock, the food she'd just eaten resting like lead in her stomach. *Was* she wrong? Suddenly it seemed as if having a child was a luxury she couldn't afford—worse, something she had no right to. Despite the desert heat, the blood in her veins ran cold.

Adam led the paint over to her and mounted his Appaloosa. "Do you want to stay in this area for the next couple of days?" he asked.

Sierra nodded. She grasped the reins and swung into the saddle.

"I'd like to ride down the trail and find a base camp. We need fresh water for the horses. We'll stay within sight of Weavers Needle."

Adam's voice was impersonal again, the voice of a hired guide, and Sierra responded in kind.

"That'll be fine."

She rode behind him, trying to whip up her confidence again. Maybe Adam was mistaken. After all, he only had a guide's knowledge of the area. She was the historian. No matter what, she decided with new resolve, she wasn't going home until she found the mine. She'd prove Adam wrong yet. Or would it be the other way around?

The rest of the afternoon left little time for thinking. Adam chose a site for their base camp, just north of Weavers Needle and south of Black Top Mountain. It provided shade, some sparse grass and mesquite, and a small pool of water that would last the horses a few days.

Sierra busied herself first with comparing maps, then scouting for promising landmarks. Her plan was simple: review Jacob Waltz's descriptions, find all the landmarks on the old maps she'd researched beforehand and correlate them with the new. Once she did that, she'd know exactly where to look for the Lost Dutchman Mine. She pushed aside all thoughts of the earthquake. How much of a difference could one little earthquake mean? Arizona wasn't California, with its massive faults and quakes.

Adam remained at her side. His disapproving attitude gradually relaxed and he answered all her questions. He even assisted in her search for landmarks. Sierra hoped his apparent change of heart wasn't motivated by pity. Still, at least he was living up to his part of the bargain. She decided to hike as far as she could up Black Top Mountain—not an easy task, considering the broken spires and loose rock.

It was late in the day when she finally stopped her ascent, Adam beside her. She took some more pictures and studied the maps. Suddenly a hand reached under her nose to pull the map away. Sierra glanced up in surprise.

"You're missing the view. Try looking at it with an eye toward beauty, not treasure."

Sierra did. The spires were splintered and jagged, but many still stretched toward the clouds with an ageless dignity. She drew in a deep breath, reveling in the sight of jagged bronze rocks and the vast desert they overshadowed.

"What's that large formation to the south?" Sierra asked. "Isn't it west of where we picked up the Peralta trail?"

"Yes. That whole rock formation is Superstition Mountain, which gives its name to this range. You didn't get a good look at it because we drove right up to the base."

"What would I have seen?"

"There's a chalk cliff shaped like a great wave ready to break. It's part of a limestone ledge."

Adam pointed to the distant south. "You can't see it from this angle, but the other cliffs on the front of the mountain have rock formations shaped like humans."

"Strange rock formations seem to be the rule rather than the exception here."

"True. But the Pima Indians had a myth about these particular ones. A long time ago there was a great flood and the people climbed to the top of the cliffs to escape the rising waters. They fought with each other, each selfishly trying to reach the safest spot. The Pima god grew angry. He stopped the flood, but turned the people to stone. According to the story, that's where the frozen white wave and the humanlike rocks came from."

"I'd like to get some pictures of the formation for our book."

"Good idea. That area's a beautiful part of the mountains." Adam's voice warmed with enthusiasm. "Most people miss it because it's on the outside of the entrance to the Superstitions. We could backtrack now if you want."

"I'd like that, Adam, but I don't think I can afford the time away from my..."

"Treasure hunt?"

Sierra flushed. "My work. I'm on a tight schedule. You understand, don't you?"

"I understand all too clearly." The animation left his face. "It's getting late. I don't want us descending in the dark," he said. "Let's go."

Sierra took one last look around, then followed him. Their descent was made in silence. One of the horses nickered a greeting, then went back to grazing.

"What would you like to eat?" Adam asked.

"What I'd really like is for you to stop talking to me in that disapproving voice."

"You know how I feel about treasure hunters."

"I know. We rank only above single women who want to adopt. So you've said. Not that I have a chance of success in either, according to you." Sierra stowed her camera and notebook away with jerky motions. "It's becoming tiresome. I wish you'd stop bringing it up."

"I've treated you with every courtesy and I'm..." Adam took a step toward her, but Sierra averted her face. "Sierra, are you crying?"

"Of course not." She dashed away her tears with a furious hand. "I'm angry. There's a difference." She checked to make sure she had fresh film for the morning. "Go eat."

"I don't want to eat. I want to talk to you! Isn't that what we agreed? I've fulfilled my part of the bargain by helping you search for the mine, haven't I?" He laid a calming hand on her shoulder, but Sierra shook it off.

"In addition to doing everything you can to discourage me," she accused him, "like regaling me with stories about dead prospectors—not to mention old earthquakes. I don't appreciate it one bit."

Adam's eyes narrowed. "Every word has been the truth, which is more than you can say."

Sierra gasped indignantly. "You've called me a liar once too often, Adam Copeland." She grabbed her gear and retreated to the tent. She couldn't let him know she was more angry with herself than with him. If the man had any tact at all, he wouldn't follow her.

He did.

He opened her tent flap and peered in. "I'm only worried about your safety."

"No, you aren't. You're only worried about stopping me from adopting." Sierra immediately exited again, Adam right on her heels. She spun around to face him. "All right, so I told one lie. I admit it. I've said I'm sorry. But I want children. What's wrong with that? Who are you to judge me?"

"I'm no judge." Adam reached for her arms and pulled her close. "But I am your guide, and I'm not going to let you get hurt in these mountains."

"Now that's a switch!" Sierra couldn't believe what she was hearing. "Since when did you stop treating me like a customer and actually realize I'm a person?"

"Since now," he said, and he brought his mouth down hard on hers.

CHAPTER SIX

ADAM'S LIPS DEMANDED a response—a response that Sierra chose to make. Suddenly she was acutely aware of everything: the warmth of the setting sun on her back, the smell of the creosote bushes, and the feel of Adam's body against her.

Even when he finally released her, that awareness remained. Sierra wondered if her world would ever again be the same. She brought her fingertips up to her lips and lightly traced where his had been.

"I'm not going to apologize for that," Adam said hoarsely. He shoved his hands into his pockets, as if he couldn't trust himself not to touch her.

"I'm not asking you to," she replied quietly. This was not the tender kiss of earlier. This was a kiss of passion, of fierce possession.

Sierra kept her gaze on Adam. She desperately wanted to know what he was thinking, what he was feeling. For that matter, she wished she could sort out her own confused feelings. She'd been kissed before, but no one else had even come close to making her so aware of herself as a woman.

Adam started to say something, stopped, then started again. "Just consider it the Superstitions weaving their spell."

"Is that what it was?" Sierra had the distinct impression that he meant to say something else. "Nothing more?"

Adam shrugged lightly and seemed to regain some of his lost composure. "As a guide, I suppose I get too concerned about the people I'm responsible for—especially clients with crazy notions like yours."

Sierra continued to study him. The acute awareness she still felt told her Adam was lying. But why? He'd already made clear his low opinion of her. Was he feeling guilty about being physically attracted to someone he couldn't respect?

She closed her eyes. That thought hurt. The pain chased away the sensation that time was standing still for them. The magic disappeared. When she opened her eyes, Sierra was herself again. She saw that Adam hadn't moved.

"You'd better go eat before it gets dark. I'm not hungry. I'm going to work on my notes," she mumbled.

Adam said nothing, but Sierra could feel his eyes follow her all the way into her tent.

She sat cross-legged on her sleeping bag, ignoring the dusty marks her boots left on the material. She tossed her hat to the ground and picked up her notes. But it was almost impossible to concentrate on them. Adam filled her every thought.

There was no room for her in Adam's life, she warned herself. He was a law unto himself, a solitary man of the desert. She instinctively knew that when Adam really wanted something, he'd want all or nothing. And her woman's instincts told her that Adam wanted her—as she wanted him. But she could give him only a part of herself. She had other dreams, other commitments. Was that why he'd withdrawn from her?

Sierra sighed. She was already half in love with the man. But she wanted children, and home and hearth just didn't fit with his lonely existence in the desert, no matter how much she might wish they did.

It was much later when Sierra finally finished her work. She'd taken photographs and made detailed notes describing most of the places she and Tony had agreed on. A few more photos and a little more research would complete her task. Now it was time to work on her own project.

She carefully studied her maps. Sierra was certain she'd worked out the precise location of the mine, despite what Adam had told her about the earthquake. Her observations today from Black Top Mountain had only confirmed her feelings. She was so close. All she needed was one more day to find the Lost Dutchman. She'd document her findings, call in the press, take her bows, and then go home to await that staff position and her child.

Somehow the prospect of leaving Adam—going home—didn't make for a good night's rest. She was still awake hours later when she heard him at her tent flap.

"Sierra? Are you decent?"

"Just a minute." Sierra groped for the flashlight beside her and turned it on. Then she climbed out of the sleeping bag and pulled on her shirt and jeans. "All right, come on in."

Adam unzipped the flap, letting in a rush of cold air. He grabbed her boots, shook them out and handed them to her. "Here. Get these on, and hurry."

Sierra looked up in alarm. "What's wrong?" she asked as she reached for her socks.

"There's a big thunderstorm headed this way. We've got to get out of here—fast."

"Are you sure it's a storm front and not just the wind?" Sierra asked. She could see the tent sides billowing.

"Yes. The horses are so nervous they're trying to pull out the picket lines and run."

Sierra hurried her movements. A smart camper never doubted animal instincts when it came to weather.

"Where are we headed?" she asked as she began to roll up her sleeping bag.

Adam started rolling the ground cloth. "As far out of here as we can get. I—"

His words were drowned out by a booming clap of thunder. One of the horses screamed, and Adam dropped the ground cloth.

"Forget the sleeping bag. Grab your bags and saddle. I've got to get to the horses."

"What about the tent?" Sierra asked in confusion.

"Leave it! We're getting the hell out of here!"

Sierra was alarmed at the urgency of his voice. She threw on her denim jacket, slung the saddlebags over her shoulders and lifted the saddle, carrying it in her arms. The wind hit her square in the face and as she left the tent. Adam was holding the horses. Both were prancing nervously, their manes flying wildly about their necks. The Appaloosa was already saddled.

"Can you see to saddle the paint in the dark?" Adam had to yell to be heard above the wind.

"Yes." She could, just barely. The clouds were moving fast, but here and there the moonlight still showed through.

A flash of lightning and another clap of thunder exploded northeast of them. The paint reared, nostrils flaring, but Sierra already had the bridle and bit on him.

"Whoa!" she ordered, jumping back to avoid an iron-shod hoof.

Adam tightened his grip on the halter lead as Sierra struggled with the saddle. Finally it was secured on Spot's back, and the reins were in her hand. The wind blew in heavier and heavier gusts, and suddenly Sierra's tent flew through the air. The Appaloosa jumped, the paint kicked with fright, and Adam fought to avoid losing them.

"Sierra, can I let go of Spot yet? I can barely hold my horse as it is." Adam's feet scrambled to keep pace with his panicky horse as he reeled in the lead. "Can you mount up on your own?"

"Yes, go! I'll follow."

The paint's hooves skittered on the desert floor, but Sierra managed to put a foot in one stirrup and swing into the saddle. The horse tried to bolt. His front legs left the ground in protest as Sierra pulled back hard on the reins.

Adam was having more trouble getting control of the stallion, but finally he, too, was in the saddle. Another flash of lightning illuminated the narrow canyon. Sierra watched Adam's hat fall down his back, then blow into the canyon as the storm's power broke the chin strap.

She grabbed the saddle pommel for security as the lightning flashed, knowing that Spot would surely react. The thunder exploded and bounced back and forth between the canyon walls. Her leg muscles tensed as her mount reared once more. Sierra fought to calm him.

She searched for Adam and saw he'd found the trail in the dark. She forced the trembling paint to follow the bigger horse. Another clap of thunder boomed. The shrill clarion cry of the Appaloosa echoed in the canyon, and then the horses were off and running.

The canyon was black except for the sporadic flashes of light. The horses flew at top speed, turning, twisting and jumping over a trail Sierra couldn't even see. There was no question of guiding her horse, no question of controlling his speed. All Sierra could do was pray that she or Adam wouldn't fall, and hang on for the fastest wildest ride of her life.

The wind grew colder, bringing with it the smell of rain. The lightning increased so much that all Sierra could see now was bright spots and streaks. It was as if someone had popped a camera's flash over and over in front of her eyes. The horses didn't slacken their frantic pace. Sierra closed her eyes against the coarse mane lashing at her face, but riding without sight was too frightening and she immediately opened them again.

One flash of lightning showed Adam ahead of her, twisted around in the saddle, desperately searching for her in the dark. Sierra felt an icy stab of fear. He was risking his balance by turning like that when his horse was at full gallop. Adam was no greenhorn. Didn't he know any better?

"Turn around!" she screamed at him. She felt an overwhelming relief when her voice reached his ears and he did just that.

Sierra was gasping. She didn't know how long they'd been riding, but she was breathless with the effort of holding on. Was it minutes? Hours? In the dark she wasn't sure where she was, but her sense of navigation told her they were far from their original camp.

Her muscles quivered with the strain of keeping her balance. She was exhausted from the pounding pace of the gallop. She had to rest. She tried pulling up on the reins, but the paint shook his head and took the bit between his teeth. Then the rain began to fall, hard stinging darts of water were driven painfully against bare skin by the force of the wind. Sierra heard the Appaloosa scream again. After that the rain drowned out everything except the sound of hooves on rock.

Dear Lord, how could the horses see where they were going? Sierra thought. How could anyone see?

But Adam seemed to know where they were. He finally managed to slow his horse, and Sierra struggled to do the same. The animals were still frightened, but their wild running had winded them badly. The gallops became canters, then jerky trots as Adam guided them with a reassuring certainty. It wasn't until they were almost upon a building that Sierra was able to recognize a shack in the rain-filled darkness.

She nearly collapsed then and there with relief.

"Don't get down!" Adam yelled. He dismounted, tied his horse, then came back and took the reins from her. He led her horse around the tiny building to the side most sheltered from the wind. When he'd tied the paint next to the Appaloosa at the cabins' hitching post, he grasped her by the waist and lifted her down.

Sierra kicked her feet out of the stirrups with limp trembling muscles. Adam's arms were tight around her, and he half dragged, half carried her into the cabin. He kicked the door closed behind him, and they both collapsed onto the floor, breathless, exhausted—but alive.

The rain dripped off Sierra's body and made dirty puddles on the dusty linoleum. Sporadic flashes of lightning revealed that the shack was no bigger than a small bedroom, with only a desk, two battered chairs and a gas lamp. But it was dry and out of the wind, and for that, Sierra was grateful.

As her breathing gradually slowed, she became aware that Adam's arms were still clasped about her waist, his hard chest against her back. But she was too exhausted to move, and by the rapid rise and fall of his chest, she knew Adam was just as drained.

"Are you all right?" he finally asked. He shifted her around to face him, pushing back the soggy strands of hair plastered to her forehead.

"I feel like I'm still riding a horse," she gasped. "Either that or my heart's in overdrive. The ground's still moving." Sierra shivered and felt Adam's arms tighten around her.

"Thank God you're in one piece." Adam leaned his cheek against her wet hair. Her hat had blown off long ago. "I was so afraid you'd fall."

"Not me. I never fall." Sierra managed to shake her head. "If you fell back home, you got trampled by cattle. But I was worried about you."

"Me?"

Another clap of thunder rattled the windows of the tiny building, followed by a flash of brightness.

Sierra took a deep breath. "You could have fallen, Adam. You turned around while your horse was at a full gallop. Why? You know how dangerous that is."

Adam gave her a straight answer. "I couldn't go on without knowing you were still behind me."

"I *told* you I could ride a horse!" Her pent-up fear for his safety finally burst free. "You could have broken your neck! Scaring me half to death, as if I wasn't scared enough already! I could just...just..."

"Just what?" Adam's voice was as unsteady as hers.

"Oh, Adam." Sierra buried her head on his shoulder, hugging him hard. "Thank goodness your horse has some sense, or else I'd be back there picking up what was left of you on the rocks!"

"Sierra." Adam drew her head away from his shoulder and held it lovingly between his hands. "Sierra, I'm all right. Don't tell me you're becoming hysterical. Next you'll probably start crying on me."

"No, I won't." Sierra felt his arms drop to her waist to pull her closer. "But if you ever pull such a foolish stunt again, you'll be sorry. I'll give you such a piece of my mind that—"

"Sierra, be quiet." And he covered her lips with his.

Sierra thought she'd never experienced anything so heavenly as that kiss. She wanted more, and she knew that Adam did, too, but their exhaustion extinguished the flame that tried to spring into life.

Adam didn't try to sit up. In fact, he slumped back against the wall, pulling Sierra with him.

"My boots are wet," she said, her voice almost a wheeze. "Inside and out."

"Mine, too." Adam took in deep gulps of air, as did she. "But they can wait. Just rest, Sierra."

They were quiet as they relaxed. Sierra felt the warmth of his body and knew a sweet and unfamiliar comfort. Physically and emotionally, Adam aroused something deep within her. If only she didn't have so many other pressing matters to take care of! Then she could welcome Adam into her heart....

After a while he said, "I should go out to the horses and get the saddlebags. At least we could change into dry clothes."

Another clap of thunder shook the very foundations of the cabin. Sierra grabbed Adam's hands and held them tight. "Don't go outside. I'd rather catch cold than have you get struck by lightning. Maybe we can find some blankets in here."

"Good idea. I'm not really keen on going out there while it's still pouring."

He gently moved Sierra to a place against the wall, then stood up. He fumbled in the dark until he found the gas lantern, then pumped it up and lit it with the automatic starter.

The steady light illuminated their surroundings. "That's better. Thank goodness this didn't need matches," he said, looking around the room.

Sierra made no effort to stand. She didn't think she could trust her legs just yet.

"There aren't any blankets. But there's instant coffee and a gas burner, so we can make ourselves a hot drink. And there's a phone on the desk." Adam reached gingerly over the desk, trying not to drip too much water on the surface.

"Is it working?"

Adam listened, then replaced the receiver. "No. I'll try again later."

Sierra sat up a little straighter and looked out the window. "What is this place?"

"We're at a ranger checkpoint cabin."

"Is anyone supposed to be here?"

Adam shook his head. "These little cabins are only manned during the peak camping season."

"What about the phone? Is it turned off for the season, or is it out because of the storm?"

Adam turned on the tiny burner and warmed his hands. "I don't know. Whatever the case, let's pray we get a dial tone later. I need to call Weldon and have him meet us with the horse trailer."

Sierra paused in the middle of taking off one very soggy boot. "Meet us? I don't want to leave now! I need to finish my research! And I need one more day to find the Lost Dutchman!"

"Sierra, don't be ridiculous. Look outside. This could last hours—days! It's too dangerous to stay."

Another clap of thunder underlined his words.

"Would you . . . would you still be my guide once the weather's cleared?" Sierra asked.

Adam looked up sharply.

"I don't have anyone else," she went on. "I know this is a wild-goose chase to you, but it's much more than that to me." Sierra couldn't see Adam's face as he bent to pull off her other boot. He balanced them upside down against the wall before answering. "Why not? Who knows? Maybe you'll prove the whole world wrong, after all."

Despite her wet clothing, suddenly she didn't feel so chilled anymore. "Thank you, Adam."

He frowned. "Don't thank me yet. I have to get us out of here first. You stay put. I need to go outside and check on the horses, and I'll get our bags. I also have to bring in some water if we want coffee. There's none in here."

"You be careful." Sierra finally stood up, gazing into the darkness outside. The wind wasn't as bad as before, but the rain was like a waterfall. She'd never seen anything like it. She waited anxiously until Adam returned.

"How are the horses?" she asked.

"Miserable, but there's nothing we can do about that. There's not enough room in here to bring them in." He placed her saddlebags beside her. "I don't know how dry the clothes will be, but anything has to be better than what we're wearing now.''

He rummaged in his own bags. "My sleeping bag is dry. We can spread it on the floor for tonight. After seeing what happened to your tent, I don't think either one of us wants to sleep outside."

"Where am I supposed to change?" Sierra asked.

"Right here. I'll turn my back, and you do the same for me. I'll put the water on to boil. Let me know when you're ready."

Sierra pulled on another long sleeved western shirt. She hurried to fasten it, the metal of the front rivets cold against her chest, then added dry underwear and a pair of jeans. "Okay. I'm finished. Your turn."

Sierra rolled up her wet clothes and placed them in a corner. There was no sense in putting them in her bags. They'd only get her other things wet. Adam changed while Sierra wiped out two dusty cups with a paper napkin and prepared the coffee.

"It's only instant, but it'll warm us up," she said, handing Adam a cup.

Sierra took her place on one wooden chair, Adam on the other. She tucked her bare feet on the chair rung, away from the wet floor. They drank in silence, the pounding of the rain and the whistling of the wind the only sounds. When Adam finished he rose and unpacked his ground cloth and sleeping bag, then spread them on the floor.

He stretched himself out on top, leaving her a free half. "We haven't had much rest tonight. You'd better try to get some sleep."

"After I finish my coffee."

Adam gave her a knowing smile. "Don't be nervous, Sierra. Even though I'm sorely tempted to kiss you again, I'm too tired to try. Turn off the lamp when you're ready to come to bed." Adam threw his arm over his eyes and was asleep within minutes.

Sierra watched him sleep, feeling protective, content and restless all at the same time. She was going to miss Adam when she left. She discovered that, in many ways, they were very much alike. They were both passionate people when it came to their beliefs.

If only she could stay. But she couldn't, not if she was going to see through her commitments. Not if she wanted to adopt a child. Luckily, *Southwest History* was based in Phoenix, much closer to Adam. Now she had another reason, a very important one, for wanting to find the lost mine.

On impulse Sierra checked her watch—4:00 a.m.— and picked up the phone again. She was too wound up to sleep, and she suddenly felt a desperate need to get through to her hotel and check her messages. A need, somehow, to reestablish contact with the world she'd left behind.

Miraculously, there was a dial tone. Sierra immediately dialed Weldon's number, which she'd memorized. Better to call Weldon now and arrange for transportation tomorrow in case the storm continued.

The call went right through.

"Hello, Weldon? This is Sierra Vaughn. I'm sorry to wake you, but..." Sierra quickly filled Weldon in on the situation.

"I'll get out there as soon as the storm's over," Weldon said, "but I can't guarantee when that'll be. Sometime tomorrow, weather permitting."

"Thanks, I'll tell Adam. And good night."

Sierra breathed a sigh of relief. That was one worry out of the way. Then she tried her hotel. The phone was answered on the fifth ring.

"Saguaro Inn."

"Hello, this is Sierra Vaughn, room 103. I'd like to check for any messages, please."

"Oh, yes, Ms. Vaughn. I have a few here. Just a minute," said the woman at the reception desk. "A Tony Miller called. He said to tell you your publisher moved up your deadline, and he needs all your notes and photos by the end of this week at the latest."

Sierra scribbled in her notebook. "Got it. Anything else?"

"A Mr. Rydell called."

"Mr. Rydell?" He was from the Colorado adoption agency!

"Yes. That's R-Y-D—"

"I know how to spell it," Sierra interrupted in her excitement. "What did he say?"

"He said to tell you he had a child ready for you to adopt."

"For *me?*" Sierra almost danced with joy. "Go on."

"He said you had to be in his office to sign the papers by Friday morning."

Friday? It was 4:00 a.m. Thursday now! That meant she had today to find the Dutchman and tomorrow to finish her notes and hop a flight back home. That didn't leave her much time.

"Are you sure he said *this* Friday? Tomorrow?" Sierra asked, grasping at straws.

"Yes. He said it had to be this Friday, or the girl would go to the next couple on the waiting list. He also wants more information on that tentative job offer you mentioned before he signs the papers."

"A girl?" Sierra felt tears in her eyes. A daughter!

"A little four-year-old named Jennifer. Congratulations, ma'am."

"Yes, thank you. Good night." Sierra hung up, shaking with excitement that soon turned to dismay.

Friday was too soon! She looked in her notebook for Mr. Rydell's number. His office had an answering machine. She would call him and explain that she might be late, as she was out of town at her publisher's request. Surely they wouldn't hold that against her, would they?

Sierra felt her tension ease. Of course they wouldn't. A few extra days was all she needed. And then, after all the waiting, she'd finally be a mother. She had a daughter! Well, almost.

Sierra picked up the phone to dial Mr. Rydell's number.

"Oh, no! No!"

The phone was dead.

Sierra took a deep breath then glanced at Adam, still sound asleep despite her loud cry of frustration. Good. The phone service would come back on in a minute. But a minute went by, and it didn't. The rain let up slightly, and she tried again. An hour went by, and still no friendly dial tone. The sun started to rise, and still nothing.

Sierra bit her lip, then made her decision. She pulled on her damp boots and grabbed her saddlebags. She looked at Adam, asleep on the floor. She didn't dare wake him, for she knew he'd try to stop her from leaving. But she should tell him about Weldon.

She wrote him a note.

"Wanted to check out one more thing. Called Weldon—he'll be at the Peralta trailhead sometime today. Will meet you there ASAP. Don't worry. Sierra."

Sierra reread her short message. She turned off the lamp and placed the note on the desk carefully anchoring it with the dead telephone. As she opened the door to step out into the rain, she took one last look at Adam's sleeping form. She hesitated, wanting to call out to him, wanting to tell him she'd be back. Then she firmly closed the door behind her.

She had a date with history. She had a date with the Dutchman.

CHAPTER SEVEN

THE RAIN CONTINUED to fall as Sierra backtracked on the paint. The wind cut through the canyon; both horse and rider felt the sting of rain in their faces. A few times the paint snorted in annoyance and tried to turn around against the wind, but Sierra kept him on course.

The sun rose, a faded gray object that couldn't dispel the rain's gloom. However, there was enough light to see. Sierra could hardly believe the obstacles she'd ridden over last night. Both she and Adam were lucky that they and the horses hadn't been injured on the rough rocky trail.

She checked her watch. It was now almost 10:30. She'd been riding all morning at a cautious pace, but another half hour should put her back at Black Top Mountain. Already she could see the peak far ahead. According to her map work, Black Top Mountain hid the Lost Dutchman mine.

Sierra frowned. It wouldn't be an easy climb, not with the wind and the rain. The ground would be slippery, but at least the thunder and lightning were gone, and she had the gloomy light of a rainy day to help her. She decided to unload her saddlebags before the climb. She'd take only her camera, binoculars and a small folding pick-and-shovel set. The rest of her gear could remain with the horse.

The wind was still strong when Sierra dismounted and picketed the horse, making certain he was as high above the soggy trail as possible. She patted his neck and rubbed his soft nose.

"We'll be back at your barn in no time," she promised him. "I'll fix you some warm bran." To think she had once thought Spot an unworthy mount. She gave him one last pat, then turned toward the mountain and began to climb.

Broken pieces of rock, from small chunks to massive slabs, littered her path. Despite her excitement, Sierra chose her footing carefully. She had no intention of breaking a leg when she was so close to the find of a lifetime.

She mentally compared her present surroundings with the maps. She'd memorized where the Dutchman should be. What had Adam had called it? Her X-marks-the-spot location. Well, this was one X that *was* going to mark the spot! The right spot.

Thinking of Adam made Sierra uneasy. She slipped a little on a loose patch. She hoped he wasn't too angry. But even if he was, he couldn't stop her—could he?

At that thought Sierra halted her climb altogether. He wouldn't come after her, she tried to convince herself. After all, she knew how to survive in the wilderness; she wasn't endangering either her own safety or the horse's. And she'd promised Adam she'd catch up with him and Weldon as soon as she'd checked this last location. Besides, no one would go out in the rain without a darn good reason. Like hers.

Sierra continued to climb, but without as much enthusiasm as before. She knew Adam would consider her an irresponsible idiot for going treasure hunting in this weather. Why couldn't he see that she was a grown woman who knew what she wanted? Those landmarks above showed how close she was to getting it.

Sierra clenched her teeth. Maybe Adam was still asleep, she thought hopefully. Or maybe he and Weldon were sitting in the pickup truck, warm and dry drinking coffee from a thermos. She stopped again and reached for the binoculars in her bags. She cupped her hand, shielding the lenses from the rain as she brought them to her eyes.

Sierra pointed the binoculars at the trail she'd just ridden and swept them up and down. With any luck, all would be well.

"Oh, no," she cried. "That's just great!" There was the Appaloosa stallion. With Adam Copeland on his back.

Sierra adjusted the focus and gave a silent whistle. Adam didn't look too happy. His jacket didn't have a hood like hers, and since he'd lost his hat, his hair was soaked. Water ran down his face and, judging by the way he was hunched forward in the saddle, down his neck, too. Sierra lowered the binoculars. She'd bet her last cent it wasn't the rain putting that angry look on Adam's face.

She tucked the binoculars inside the front of her jacket. The way she saw it, she had two choices. She could go back down to the trail and calmly wait for him, wasting a whole hour's climb. Or she could cover the scant remaining distance to her target above and find the Lost Dutchman.

Sierra made the logical choice. She put one foot in front of the other and took a step up. Then she stopped.

What if she lost his good opinion forever? She felt a sudden pang in her chest. If only she'd told Adam about the adoption agency's message in her note. Then he'd understand why she was here. She'd have to tell him herself. Maybe she'd even relent and explain that, without adoption, she'd never have a child of her own. Once he knew that, everything would be all right between them.

"I'll tell him as soon as I've found the Dutchman," she promised herself as she took another step up.

What if Adam saw her horse and was worried about her? What if he believed she was lost?

Sierra shook off that thought and took another step up. "He'll be fine," she told herself. She stopped again.

What if he was worried enough to start climbing the peak, too? What if he followed her muddy trail up the mountains, hurrying all the while? What if he slipped and fell?

"Don't be ridiculous," she told herself. She took another step up.

What if he fell and died?

Sierra moaned and closed her eyes. He wouldn't fall, she told herself. He was an experienced outdoorsman, a capable climber.

Who was she kidding? She couldn't stand the thought that he might end up hurt—or worse.

"You're just a sentimental fool," Sierra muttered aloud. *You shouldn't let yourself care about Adam Copeland.*

He thinks you're a crazy treasure hunter. He doesn't care about you.

"Damn you, Adam," she groaned. "Why can't you leave me alone?" But she turned and started going back down.

The descent was easy. Most of the time she let herself slide down the slick wet hill in a sitting position. She didn't have to hurry, but she hurried nonetheless. Adam should be reaching her horse in the next fifteen or so minutes, and she wanted to be there when he arrived. She continued to make good time down the slope.

She was more than two-thirds of the way down before she could see him clearly without benefit of the binoculars.

"Hurry up, Adam," she urged aloud. "I have a treasure to find."

Sierra saw Adam look up, as if he'd heard her. She knew that wasn't possible and wondered what had caught his attention. Seconds later she saw.

Behind horse and rider, a wall of water was rushing down the narrow canyon. The roar grew louder as the water drew nearer. Adam looked frantically around, then spurred his horse forward.

Sierra's stomach dropped with a sick lurch as she watched. There was no place for him to go! The sides of the canyon were too steep for man or horse to climb at that point in the trail. Adam couldn't make his way to higher ground until he reached the place where Sierra had picketed her horse.

Sierra threw herself forward and came careering down the base of the mountain toward the paint. She saw Adam kick his horse for more speed, but the Appaloosa was apparently exhausted.

They weren't going to make it.

The water reached Adam, and horse and rider were swept up by the current and then under.

"No!" Sierra screamed as she ran, stumbling in her haste, toward the paint.

She made it to Spot's side, but before she could scream again, Adam and the Appaloosa surfaced in different places, both fighting for air in the swirling froth. In just seconds they would rush by her.

Sierra grabbed at the pommel and removed her lariat. How many thousands of cattle had she roped? Enough to attempt the impossible and succeed?

"Please make my aim straight," she prayed as she shook out a loop. She raced to a nearby slab of rock and braced her legs against it so that the current couldn't drag her in.

She swung the rope above her head, its coil cutting through the rain. She watched Adam's black head sweep closer, closer, and her eye gauged speed and distance and she made adjustments for the wind. Just as she'd done so many times before. Only one thing was different—this time she wouldn't get another chance if she missed.

Sierra didn't feel her teeth on her lip. She didn't taste the blood. Her whole body tensed and waited as she kept her wrist circling.

Now! her instincts cried. *Now!*

The loop went sailing through the air, the sound of the flood drowning out its hiss. It flew over the water toward Adam just as the water sucked him down again.

"Adam!" Sierra shrieked as her body instinctively jerked back to pull the loop taut. Would she be reeling in an empty catch?

Sierra gasped as the weight wrenched her shoulders with a mighty tug. She had him! She sank to her knees and braced her body against the rock. The slab was now waist-high, so she still had a clear view of the flood, but she couldn't see Adam. All she could see was swirling foam.

"Adam, hang on!"

She pulled as hard as she could, the rope biting into her leather riding gloves. Adam's head rose from the water, then his hands were grabbing the lifeline.

Sierra exhaled as they both took in a tremendous gulp of air. He was alive!

Her joy soon turned to panic as she tried to pull.

"Adam, I can't haul you in!" she yelled not knowing if he could hear her over the roar of the water. "The current's too strong!"

Already her arms were trembling, and her shoulders felt as if they were being torn from their sockets. If it weren't for the rock she was kneeling behind, Sierra would have already lost her position.

Adam tried to pull himself in, only to be tossed about in the water like a rag doll. Sierra felt her heart race as she saw him go under again. Had she found him only to lose him?

She gulped in a deep breath, held it and pulled. The rope moved forward only inches at her attempt, but it was enough to bring Adam's head clear of the water. Sierra painfully took up the slack. Then she braced herself even lower and pulled again.

The rope cut deep into her palms through the wet, leather gloves. Her back arched, aching with the effort, but Adam had his hands back on the rope.

She gave a great heave, gasping at the strain to her arms. She saw Adam's eyes above the water and could have cried at the hopelessness in them. Adam was afraid he wasn't going to make it. He was tiring rapidly with the effort of fighting the current that was dragging him down into its depths.

Sierra pulled with all her strength, but she gained nothing this time. In fact, she lost ground as the force of the water pulled her to her feet. Her body was stretched across the rock, her feet barely touching the ground. Her muscles could give no more. She couldn't save him.

She knew it. Adam knew it.

His eyes never left hers as one of his hands let go of the rope. Then she saw his other hand let go. His face told her what would come next. Adam would reach to his waist, loosen the rope and slip silently away.

"Don't you do it!" Sierra struggled to regain her position behind the rock. She shook her head violently.

Adam's lips moved. Although she couldn't hear them, Sierra could read the single words. "Yes. Not you, too, Sierra."

"Don't, Adam! I love you!" Sierra screamed. She threw back her head and yanked with everything that was in her. She'd haul him in or die trying.

Her feet regained their foothold behind the slab, and she braced them on the rock itself instead of the ground. Her neck muscles stood taut with strain.

She couldn't do this inch by inch, she realized with deadly clarity. She couldn't last that long. Neither could Adam. She'd have to haul him in with one final effort.

Please let me do this, she silently prayed. *Just let me save him and I'll never ask for anything again.*

Sierra gritted her teeth and threw her body back in a mighty heave. She felt three things at once—the ground slamming into her back, a snap in her roping arm and slackening of her line. Was Adam on shore, or had the water claimed him? Either way, her line was free.

Sierra gave a violent shudder. She tried to move and would have screamed aloud if she'd had any strength left. The pain in her arm was excruciating. She didn't care, not if Adam was all right.

Please make him be all right. I love him. I don't want to live without him.

She couldn't bring herself to turn her head and look toward the flood's bank. The agony of not knowing would be nothing compared to seeing Adam gone. She tried to call out his name, but it was an effort just to breathe, let alone speak. She closed her eyes.

The rain on her face stopped, but she could still hear it falling all around her. Confused, Sierra opened her eyes and looked up.

"Adam?"

His dear head was stopping the rain from reaching her.

Adam nodded. His face was white, but he was alive and whole. He tenderly brushed her rain-slick cheek.

"Don't move, sweetheart. Your arm..." His voice broke as he looked down at the crazy angle no normal arm could ever have.

Sierra gave him the faintest of smiles. "I have a great arm. Didn't I tell you? My brothers could never out-rope me." She closed her eyes again.

"Sierra? Sierra!"

Sierra didn't answer.

THE RAIN HAD FINALLY STOPPED when Sierra regained consciousness. She was lying on the ground, her head on something soft, her arm strapped to her chest. It was still daylight, she realized, for she could see the over-hang of the ledge above her.

"Adam?"

"Right here." His hand squeezed her free one and went on holding it. "You're on my lap."

"Oh." Sierra blinked, trying to clear her vision.

"Do you remember what happened?" Adam asked gently.

"The flood." She moved, then froze at the pain. "My arm."

"It's broken, Sierra. I splinted it as best I could. Try not to move it."

Sierra nodded. She didn't want to do anything to increase the stabbing pain. In soft, even strokes, Adam's fingers brushed her forehead.

"Are you all right?" she asked.

"Yes."

Sierra breathed a sigh of relief. "My horse?"

"He's fine."

The memory of the flood came rushing back. "And yours?"

Adam shook his head slightly. "I don't know."

"Didn't you look for him?" Sierra asked.

"And leave you alone? No. Besides, you saw that wall of water."

She nodded, tears springing to her eyes. She knew there wasn't much hope for Adam's prize stallion.

"I'm sorry, Adam."

Adam said nothing. Then, "The water's receding. In a little while it'll be shallow enough for us to start back. Do you think you can ride?"

Sierra looked up uneasily as Adam continued stroking her forehead. She honestly didn't know if she could, and her expression said as much.

"I know it's scary, but there's no other way out."

Just thinking about moving her arm made her feel sick to her stomach. "Can't you just leave me here and go for help?"

"No. The thunderheads are building again. We're in for more flooding, and I don't think you'll be safe for long. Do you think you can sit up?"

"I'll try." Sierra did. Immediately it felt as if some-one had hurled red-hot knives at her arm. Her face turned whiter than it already was, and Adam lowered her again.

"Don't move. Take deep breaths. Sierra, don't pass out on me! I can't get you up on the horse without your help, and what with the slick footing, I can't carry you out of here. The trail's still under three feet of water."

"You shouldn't have come after me." Sierra closed her eyes and tried to ignore the pain in her arm. "Why didn't you wait for me at the ranger cabin?"

"You left in the middle of a storm to look for a non-existent treasure," Adam said in a weary voice. "What did you expect me to do?"

"I didn't expect you to nearly drown," she whispered.

Sierra felt Adam's arms tighten around her.

"I didn't, thanks to you."

"No. But you could have." Suddenly she remembered something. She opened her eyes again and shifted in Adam's arms so that she could see his face. "Adam, I have to go back. I have to find the Dutchman," she said frantically.

"After what just happened to you? Sierra, you have a broken arm! You're probably in shock. We're miles from the nearest doctor. And you want to go treasure hunting?"

"Yes." Sierra struggled to sit up again, but Adam's strength kept her down. "I called my hotel from the ranger shack. The adoption agency has a child waiting for me. It's a little girl, Adam! I have to be home by to-morrow. That means I need to find the mine today!"

"Don't move, damn it! Your arm's held together by a bandanna and a few pieces of flimsy wood. It was all I could find."

"You don't understand!" Sierra cried. "If I don't find the mine, I probably won't get that staff job. Without a regular income, I won't get my child. I have to go!"

"No. I wish you could, Sierra, but you can't."

"Please, Adam! What about my deadline? If I don't finish my notes, I'll miss it. I'll have to return my advance, and it's already spent. I'll ruin my reputation as a researcher and I'll never find work again. And then they'll take me off the adoption list for good. You have to let me go!"

Adam held her tightly or she would have risen to her feet, despite the pain. "Not in a million years," he said in a voice filled with a compassion Sierra was too upset to hear.

"I have a daughter waiting. They'll give her to the next people on the list. If you won't let me find the Dutchman, would you go for me? I have my maps." Sierra was almost sobbing. "And I'll tell you where to look!"

"Sierra, even if I was crazy enough to climb a mountain in the rain, do you honestly think I'd leave you here all alone?" Adam's voice incredulous.

"Please. I'll be fine. Just fine," Sierra promised. "I won't move a muscle until you get back."

"*If* I get back. What happens if it starts flooding again?"

"It won't. It won't."

"It will, but we won't be here because we're both leaving, and that's final."

Tears spilled from Sierra's eyes. "You can't make me go with you. If you'd left me alone, I'd have found the mine by now. I was almost there when I saw you on the trail and came back down to meet you."

Adam studied her carefully. "Is that when you saw the flood, Sierra?"

"No. If I'd waited that long, I never would've reached my lariat in time." Sierra shivered. If she hadn't come back when she did, Adam would be dead.

Adam's eyes bored down into hers. "If I wasn't in any danger when you saw me, why did you turn back, Sierra? Why—when you had what you wanted within your reach?"

"I..." She hesitated. "I wanted to tell you about the message from the adoption agency. I didn't want you to think I was a total idiot."

"Is that all?" he asked urgently. Sierra felt his whole body tense.

What could she say to him? That she'd died a thousand deaths inside when he was trapped in that wall of water? That she wanted more than just his respect and admiration—that she wanted his love?

But Adam had given up on love when he'd exiled himself in the desert. Adam didn't have time for love, and Sierra wouldn't live without it. She couldn't. She'd done without it for too long.

"I..."

Sierra couldn't tell him the truth. Her own family had rebuffed her advances and affections too many times. Tony Miller had rejected her. And every time Adam called her a treasure hunter, he did the same. She couldn't take that again, not from Adam. So she gave him lies instead.

"I didn't want you to follow me up the mountain. I wanted to be alone when I found the treasure. That's why I came back down."

Adam exhaled slowly. Sierra didn't see the look of pain in his eyes, and when he spoke again, it was in that formal guide's voice she hated.

"I'm going to check on the water level." He carefully eased out from under her, then took off his jacket and placed it beneath her head. "If it's low enough for us to leave, I'll bring the horse in as close as I can for you."

"It's still raining. Don't you want your jacket? Adam? Adam?"

But Adam just walked away, his head bowed under the weight of the rain.

CHAPTER EIGHT

THE RIDE BACK to the Peralta trailhead seemed to take forever. Adam led the paint through knee-high water while Sierra rode. She gripped the pommel with her good hand, bracing her throbbing arm, protecting it against the slow jarring movements of the horse. A few times she came close to losing her seat, but Adam was always there to steady her.

He kept up her spirits with song as the long pain-filled hours passed. His rich baritone soothed her with songs of the desert. Sierra was grateful, and concentrated on the music to take her mind off the pain. She even tried to smile once in a while to reassure him. She knew Adam was worried sick about her. She'd been in his place herself, years before when her brother was attacked by the grizzly. She'd had to lead Jon back to the ranch on her horse. Only then she wasn't walking through a flooded trail as Adam was, but a snowy one.

Her mind clung to that memory and kept replaying it over and over. Sierra even responded to Adam's query with the wrong name.

"What did you say, Jon?" She looked down at Adam, confused. Where was she? "What happened to the snow?"

"Sierra, I'm not Jon. It's Adam, remember?"

"Where's my gun? Watch out! I see the bear!" She fumbled with her saddle, looking for the rifle she's always had to carry back home. She swayed and would have fallen if Adam hadn't caught her.

"Run, Jon, run!" She tried to scream but could only whisper the words.

She saw Adam—or was it Jon?—stop the horse and climb up behind her. He was careful not to jar her arm as he reached around to adjust the reins.

Sierra twisted her head to look at him. "Where's your horse? Is he hurt bad? Did the bear get him?" *He looks so worried,* she thought.

"Lean back against my chest, Sierra, and close your eyes. I'm okay. Everything's okay."

"I don't feel very good," she moaned, but she did as he requested. "I want to lie down."

"I know. Soon, sweetheart. Soon."

Sierra felt his lips press against her head. Why was Jon kissing her hair? He never did that. He always kissed her cheek.

"I don't want to go home," Sierra fretted. "Dad will be so mad. I lost us a steer and a horse. And my rope, too. I'll get yelled at."

"Don't worry, I have your rope," came the soothing words.

"But the horse is dead. And the steer, too, right?" Suddenly she was twelve years old again, and she started trembling. "I'll get in trouble. Dad cares more about those stupid animals than me."

"Your father loves you, Sierra. Believe me."

"He does not. Mom and Dad don't want us home. They hate us. That's why they send us out with the herd all the time, so we won't be around."

"I'm sure that's not true," Adam said, his eyes mirroring her pain.

"It is! Other kids get to stay home with their parents. They don't have to do scary things. They don't have to watch things die. I'll never do that to my kids. I wish I was someone's else's daughter. I do!" She would have burst into tears, but somehow she didn't have the energy to do anything except hurt deep inside.

Sierra felt the man kiss her again. Then he said, "Sierra, if you stay very quiet, I promise not to let your father yell at you. I'll tell him it's all my fault, okay?"

"I..." Sierra nestled against his chest. He felt warm. "Okay." Would it ever stop raining? What happened to the snow? "I'm so cold. Are we home yet?"

"Almost. Now just rest."

Sierra tried, but her arm hurt more and more. She forced her eyes open, trying to figure out where she was. She wanted to ask Jon if he knew where they were, but it was too much effort. The rain kept falling, and the horse seemed to be going slower and slower.

She must have passed out, because the sound of familiar voices woke her.

"Hand her to me, Adam."

"You be damn careful, Weldon."

Was that voice Adam's? Sierra couldn't believe he'd talk to Weldon so harshly. She struggled to open her eyes.

"Can't we get an ambulance in here?" Adam's voice contrasted with his gentle touch as he lowered Sierra from the horse into Weldon's arms.

"No," a ranger was saying. "The dirt roads in are flooded, and it's too windy for a medi-chopper. Even with his four-wheel drive, I'm surprised your friend made it in."

"The roads are terrible, Adam," Weldon agreed.

The ranger pointed toward Weldon's truck. "You'll never make it out with that horse trailer. Best leave it and your mount with me."

Sierra's arm was jolted and she cried out. She saw that she was back at the entrance to the Superstitions. The mountains, their color muted to a dull bronze by the rain, loomed above her.

"Adam?" She reached for him with her good arm.

"I'm right here. We're going to get you into Weldon's truck and then to a hospital."

"I have to find the Dutchman! I've got to go back!" she cried.

Adam ignored her. He climbed into the back passenger seat of the oversize cab and took her from Weldon's arms.

"I didn't finish my assignment!"

"Close the door, Weldon."

"I'll lose that staff job!"

"Better that than your life."

"What about my daughter? She's waiting for me!"

Weldon turned on the ignition.

"What about your horse? Don't you want to go look for him?" she asked.

"Don't talk, Sierra. Try to keep quiet."

"Please, Adam," Sierra begged. "Adam?"

Adam tightened his arms around her and laid his cheek on her head.

"Drive, Weldon."

The truck made a wide circle as Weldon headed toward the highway. For the first time Sierra noticed Superstition Mountain's rocky limestone wave, crested and ready to break. The stone people stood frozen beneath it, waiting for their destruction.

Sierra thought of all she had lost—lost through her own fault. Her trip into the Superstitions had started with a lie and had ended with a lie. She hadn't told the truth to Adam about either the treasure or her feelings for him. And because of that, she might very well have lost them both.

She choked back a sob as the stone people watched with blank eyes. She refused to cry. Instead, she went cold inside, so cold that for a crazy moment, she thought she, too, had turned to stone.

SIERRA HAD TO BE ADMITTED to the hospital. X rays showed that she'd broken both bones in her forearm. The swelling was so severe that her arm could only be splinted at first, while the pain required more than just a take-home bottle of pills. By the end of the third day the splint was removed. The bones were set and a conventional plaster cast applied. Sierra was discharged with a prescription for pain and instructions to return in six weeks.

"And stay out of airplanes for at least a week," the doctor warned her. "The lower pressure at high altitudes will swell your arm tissues. Your cast won't fit right and those broken bones could shift. We'd have to set them all over again."

Sierra could have wept at the words. Her last chance to make it home to straighten things out were gone. There was no time for a train or bus trip. She'd called Mr. Rydell; he had regretfully informed her that without the guarantee of a staff position with *Southwest History,* the four-year-old girl would be placed with another couple. Furthermore, he couldn't in all conscience keep Sierra on the adoption list if she was incapacitated and unable to work.

"I'm sorry, Ms. Vaughn, but until I know that this injury won't interfere with your present work as a free-lance researcher my hands are tied. I'd suggest you ask your next employer to send me verification papers as soon as you have another assignment."

Sierra hadn't argued.

Horrible as that call had been, she'd dreaded the next one even more. She'd have to tell Tony she hadn't completed the research and photography on the old water holes. She'd already sent him, by courier, the work she'd finished but the notes were rougher than usual and the film unprocessed. She doubted he'd be able to meet the deadline without the rest of her notes, and they might both be facing legal action for breach of contract. The call couldn't be delayed. And as she expected, Tony was not happy at all.

"I don't care if you are in the hospital! You'd better check yourself out and finish your work, or else we're both washed up. And don't send me a mess of hand-written notes, either. I'm going to try like hell to get us a two-week extension. Meanwhile, you'd better figure out some way to get me that stuff! I don't care how! And you thought you could find that damn mine!" As Tony slammed the receiver in her ear, Sierra felt only relief that after this, she'd never have to work with him—or even see him—again.

During her hospital stay, Sierra remained depressed about her situation, but Adam's visits had helped. He'd dropped in twice a day during visiting hours. They spoke little; she was too lethargic and in too much pain to chat. So Adam would bring out his blank music sheets and a pencil and write down his songs. He'd even hummed them for her. He didn't make her talk, but his presence was soothing, and Sierra was grateful.

It wasn't until the day of her discharge that Sierra felt up to any prolonged conversation.

"You aren't planning to fly home now, are you?" Adam asked as he walked her to his truck.

"No. The doctor said I shouldn't for a week or so. Besides, what do I have to go home to?" She couldn't keep the bitterness out of her voice. "I suppose I'll stay at the hotel for a while."

"You won't be going back to the hotel."

Sierra stared at him in amazement.

"In fact, I've already picked up the rest of your things. I want you to stay at the orphanage." Adam opened the truck's passenger door.

"An orphanage full of children? After losing my daughter to someone else?" Sierra nearly choked. "That's the last place I want to be."

"I understand that you don't want to be reminded of it," Adam sympathized, "but you should stay where someone can take care of you. The nuns at the orphanage will do that, and happily."

Sierra hid the pain she felt at Adam's willingness to leave her. "I see. And where will you be?"

"I'm going back to look for my horse."

Sierra instantly felt guilty. The loss of her adopted child had pushed Adam's loss into the background.

"Adam, I feel so bad about that. But why risk your own safety? The weather's still bad. Why don't we both stay at the orphanage? Surely you don't think there's any hope of finding him, do you?"

"Probably not, but I want to know for certain."

"Then I'm coming with you," Sierra declared, forcing herself to keep the desperation from her voice. "I don't want to stay with strangers. And . . . and I need to finish my photography and notes for the book."

"You're in no shape to do that. Now get in the truck."

"No." Sierra slammed the open truck door shut with her good arm, wincing as the motion jarred her broken one. "If I ever want to adopt—" Sierra swallowed hard as she thought of the four-year-old girl she would never see "—then I need to finish that book. Tony said he'd try to get us an extension. I'm not going anywhere except back to the Superstitions."

"You need someone to take care of you," Adam insisted.

"I need a job and a salary more." They glared at one another, each unwilling to give ground. "I'm not ready to live in a tent or the back of a truck like you are."

Something close to pain flickered across his face, and Sierra immediately regretted her words. "I shouldn't have said that. I'm sorry."

"It's the truth. It's also not the point. You're going to stay at the orphanage."

"I'm *not.*"

Someone blew a car horn and yelled, "Hey, buddy, are you pulling out or aren't you?"

Adam ignored the other driver. "If you promise to stay at the orphanage, I'll finish your assignment for you."

"You'd do that for me?" Sierra felt her heart swell with relief and with love. "After everything that's happened?"

"Yes. I'm a fair photographer, and I know the water holes. I can get the job done."

Sierra leaned against the truck. "And then what?"

"Then I'll come back and get you. I'll even take you to the airport when the doctor says it's okay. But until then, you need to rest."

"You were going to do this for me all along, weren't you?" she said suspiciously.

The other driver yelled out the window. "Come on, pal, the lot's full, and I've got a checkup in ten minutes."

Adam still ignored him. "Do we have a deal?"

"Yes." Sierra climbed inside the truck. What other choice did she have?

The drive south from the hospital to Tucson took two hours. Sierra slept most of the way; she woke up as they were pulling out of Tucson.

"Where are we?" she asked groggily.

"We're about five minutes from Nogales. That's where we cross the border between Arizona and Mexico." He gave her a quick glance. "How's the arm? Do you need to stop?"

Sierra swallowed. Her mouth felt fuzzy and dry. "I could use a drink."

"I'll find a gas station."

They made a brief stop for drinks and Sierra took one of her pain pills, then they continued. The rest of the drive went quickly once they'd crossed the border checkpoint. Adam followed a narrow paved road lined with organ-pipe cactus. Soon an old Spanish-style building could be seen in the distance.

"Is that it?" Sierra asked.

Adam nodded. He drove through an ancient wrought-iron gate, then into a brick-paved courtyard where he parked the car. Sierra could hear the sounds of children when he cut the engine.

"It never changes," he said. "No matter how much time passes, this place remains the same."

"How long have you been away?" she asked, wondering how many weeks, perhaps months, had gone by since his last visit to the orphanage.

"I get down here two or three times a year, including Christmas."

"Is that all?" Sierra swiveled around to face him. "You said you had happy memories of this place."

"I said happy *childhood* memories, Sierra. Orphanages don't cater to adults. Now, come on. Let's get you settled in."

A half hour later Sierra found herself in a small but pleasant room, part of the orphanage dispensary. Sister Delores, an elderly nun, brought her pillows and a pitcher of water, then shooed Adam from the room.

She carefully propped up Sierra's arm, and laid a cooling cloth on her forehead. The orphanage had no air-conditioning, though a window looking out on the courtyard was open admitting a slight breeze.

"That should be better," Sister Delores said in soft Spanish-accented English. "Is there anything else I can get you?"

"Thank you. You could tell me where Adam is. I'd like to see him."

"He will be back soon. In the meantime, please rest."

"I'll try." Sierra lay back down again. She wasn't sleepy, but her arm was throbbing, and the pill she'd taken at the gas station wasn't helping. She decided not to argue for the time being. Once the pain subsided she'd look for Adam.

She didn't have the chance. Half an hour later the old nun was back. This time she brought a boy of about seven. Sierra smiled at him, noting his shiny black hair and missing baby teeth. He reminded her of Adam, and his shy manner, coupled with mischievous eyes, endeared him to her instantly. Like all missionary-taught children, he spoke good English.

He assisted Sister Delores in exchanging the now-warm cloth for a cool one, and he was as gentle as any experienced nurse.

"Thank you. What's your name sweetheart?"

The boy smiled. "In English, I'm Luke. We get our names from the Bible, you see."

"I know." Sierra smiled back. "Someone else told me that."

"May I get the pills from your pack and lock them up?" Sister Delores asked. "We have many young children here."

"I'll get it, Sister," Luke volunteered. He scampered across the room to hand Sierra's backpack to the nun, who took out the pain pills and slipped them into a pocket of the voluminous white robes.

"You may ask for them whenever you wish. Would you like one now?" Sister Delores asked.

"No, thank you, but I'll want one this afternoon."

"It will be brought to you with your lunch."

Luke replaced the backpack. "And I will bring the meal, if you wish," he offered. Sierra guessed the young boy saved the old nun quite a few steps.

"What would you like to eat?" Delores asked. "Adam says you dislike meat, but he didn't say if you like our local dishes. They can be spicy."

"That's not a problem. I'll eat whatever you're serving. You needn't go to any special trouble."

"Is there anything else you would like?" Sister Delores asked, Luke standing in readiness to fulfill her wishes.

"I have to use the phone for a long-distance call." She needed to speak to Tony, to find out if he'd been able to get the extension on their deadline. If so, she could tell Adam how much time he had.

"One will be brought to you before lunch."

"Thank you. And I'd still like to see Adam."

The sister nodded. "He's most eager to see you again, also. But you needed rest, so we sent him away to see some old friends. I'll pass on your request."

Luke said in conspiratorial whisper, "He didn't want to go, *señorita*, but Sister made him. Adam won't dare disobey her."

Sierra looked into the old worn face. "Sister, did you know Adam when he was a boy?"

Luke started to answer, but the older nun hushed him with a wave of her hand. There was a moment's silence.

"Yes, Miss Vaughn," she replied. "But the boy of yesterday has not grown into the man I had hoped."

Then, before Sierra could express her surprise, the nun and Luke left her alone again.

It was Adam himself who brought Sierra her lunch.

"Adam, are you all right?" she asked before she could stop herself. "I was worried."

"For someone who climbs mountains in the middle of rainstorms, I didn't think the word 'worry' was in your vocabulary," Adam mildly rebuked her as he set down her lunch tray. "Sister Delores said you needed some rest. She insisted I was in the way. I wouldn't have left if I hadn't known you were in good hands."

Sierra warmed to his concern. "I missed you."

"You should worry about yourself, Sierra. I'm fine. Eat your lunch before it gets cold. We have some things to discuss before I leave." He sat in the room's only chair.

Sierra's faint appetite disappeared. "You aren't leaving so soon, are you?"

"Of course I am. I don't want you to lose your book deal, especially since it may be a while before you can work again."

"I talked to Tony. He got us the extra time."

"That helps," Adam said. He paused, then asked in a quiet voice, "Will you be all right financially? I'd like to help out if I could."

"You'd lend money to me?" Sierra asked, touched by his generosity.

"I mean give, not lend. I don't like the thought of your struggling without an income, and I worry that you'd rather do without than ask your family for help."

"How did you know?" Sierra asked. He was right.

Sierra saw Adam study her. Finally he said, "You don't remember much of the ride out of the mountains, do you?"

"Not really. I just remember my arm hurting."

"There was more to remember than that, Sierra. You thought I was your brother, and that my horse and one of the stock had been killed by a grizzly bear."

Sierra felt a chill. Even after all this time, she never liked to think about that nightmare.

"You were delirious and very agitated. You were worried your father would punish you for the loss of the steer."

"I'd rather not talk about it," Sierra told him. "It's not a pleasant memory. What's more, it's finished and done with."

"It's not, Sierra. During the ride, you told me your parents cared more about the stock than you. Don't you remember? You said they couldn't really love you because they made you watch animals die."

Sierra tried to calm her raw nerves. "I may have believed that when I was twelve. Why bring it up now?"

"Because I think you still believe it."

Sierra shook her head angrily. "I had a broken arm, Adam. You yourself said I was in shock. You can't take my ramblings seriously."

Adam clasped her good hand with his own. "You forget, I heard you, Sierra. Injured or not, you meant every word."

"Drop it, Adam," Sierra ordered in a shaking voice. "This is none of your business."

"It is, because the past can come back to ruin the present. I don't want you making that mistake."

Sierra stared at him with disbelieving eyes. "I'm not making any mistake."

"You are, or you'd let your family help you. Look at you! You're hurt, your job is in jeopardy, and instead of turning to them, you're turning to me! Sierra, tell them—your parents—your brothers—that you need them."

"I'm sure they're too busy with their ranching to bother," she insisted.

"You're wrong. You still see your parents the same way you did as a child. Sierra, think. Your parents sent you to college, away from the ranch. Doesn't that count for anything?"

"Well..."

"They didn't force you to stay. And if they were strict with you on the ranch, that's because they didn't want you hurt. Remember, you told me how worried they got when you went riding without telling them?"

Sierra nodded, her mind whirling in confusion. Suddenly her parents didn't seem to be the ogres she'd always thought them.

"Indifferent parents wouldn't have cared. I think you were too angry to see that. And you brought that anger with you into adulthood. It's distorting your perceptions. Maybe they didn't always have the time to *tell* you they loved you, but they certainly showed it. They raised you the only way they could, on a ranch. What else could they do?"

"Nothing," Sierra realized with surprise. Adam was right.

He nodded. "You need them."

"I don't need them the way I need you!" she told him. "Don't you feel the same?"

Silence.

"Aren't you going to say something?"

Adam gave a heavy sigh. "I was afraid it might come to this. Sierra, go back home. My kind of life isn't for you. I need the desert. It's kept me fighting. But it's hardly the place to have a family. Sometimes I dream about it, but..."

His words trailed off, and Sierra reached for him. "You can still have your family, Adam. Any woman would be proud to love you. I—I already do."

Adam avoided her hands. "I don't think what you're feeling is love, Sierra. Attraction—I can't deny we have that. Perhaps pity, gratitude...loneliness."

"That's not it at all!" she cried. "I love you!"

Adam rose from the bed. "I find that hard to believe. You've been known to mix fact and fiction before."

Sierra inwardly cursed. How many times would her dishonesty return to plague her?

"All my life I've had to be honest with myself. You're a beautiful woman, and I'd be lying if I said I wasn't tempted to take what you're offering. But someone who believes in fairy tales—someone like you—isn't the woman for me."

His words sounded a death knell in Sierra's heart. Had her lies denied her the chance of ever earning Adam's trust? He was a man who didn't trust easily....

Some of her despair must have shown, because Adam's next words were gentle. "Sierra, I have to leave now. I don't have much time to get your pictures if you want to meet that deadline with the publisher. The nuns will take good care of you."

He stretched out one hand, as if to touch her cheek, then dropped it awkwardly to his side. "You take care of yourself, all right?"

"Adam, won't you believe me? I don't care about finding the Lost Dutchman anymore, or finishing my assignment or—"

"Call your family, Sierra."

"I don't want them. I want you!"

"Don't."

The single harsh word sent a chill through her veins.

"I have to go. I have pictures to take and a horse to find before the next storm."

"What about us?" she pleaded.

Adam's expression was terrible to see. It was as stark and unyielding as the desert itself.

"There is no us."

Then he was gone.

CHAPTER NINE

SIERRA'S LUNCH TRAY was taken away barely touched. When her dinner tray was also untouched, Sister Delores came to see her again.

The old nun took in Sierra's red eyes and troubled expression.

"May I stay for a moment?" she asked.

"I'm not very good company, but I'd like that," Sierra replied.

Sister Delores sat down, meticulously arranging the folds of her habit.

"Your arm?" she inquired.

"It hurts," Sierra admitted.

"But not as much as your heart?"

Sierra didn't try to deny it. "Adam is upset with me, and I'm afraid I've made it worse."

Sister Delores's sympathetic demeanor made it easy for Sierra to talk, and suddenly the whole story of their ill-fated expedition into the Superstitions came pouring out.

"Adam hates me," Sierra concluded miserably. "And I . . ."

"You love him." The nun didn't seem surprised.

"Yes." It was a relief to be able to say it to someone who believed her. "We haven't known each other long, but that doesn't matter. I care about him so very much."

"Did you tell him?"

"I tried to. He didn't believe me. I don't think he feels the same." Sierra's heart contracted with pain. "To him, I'm just a crazy treasure hunter who doesn't belong here. A woman who believes in fairy tales."

The old nun shook her head. "No, Señorita Vaughn. You're the embodiment of everything Adam wants out of life. That's why he turned away from you."

"Do you really think so?" Sierra asked hopefully, but then her face fell. "I've always wanted children, but now I want more than that. Adam would make such a good husband, such a wonderful father. We could adopt a family, perhaps even a boy like Luke. If only I could convince Adam of that."

"You can't give up. You'll have to keep trying."

Sierra rubbed her forehead in agitation. "It's not that easy. There's more. This was a long time ago, but do you remember the woman who adopted Adam and then gave him back?"

The nun's face suddenly seemed much older. "A very sad affair. I have grieved much over that. Adam loved her deeply."

Sierra gave her a tremulous smile. "He told me to put the past behind me. I've had problems with my family all my life, and Adam said I couldn't enjoy the present unless I came to terms with them."

Sister Delores nodded. "Wise words."

"Yes, but he won't do the same for me. He won't put aside our . . . misunderstandings or believe that I don't care about finding the Dutchman anymore."

"Adam can be harsh at times. His trust is hard-earned. For you to have gained it and then betrayed it . . ." The nun sighed heavily. "Adam can be most stubborn."

"I know. I wish I'd never lied. It's bad enough that Adam still thinks it's wrong for single parents to adopt. So between that and my dishonesty, I have two strikes against me." Sierra lowered her eyes. "You see, I can't have children of my own. Only I didn't tell him that, either."

The old nun searched carefully for her next words. "You told Adam you loved him, but you've lied to him once. Perhaps he is afraid to believe you."

"I would never lie about something like that!"

"Ah, but Adam doesn't know that. He tends to see things in black or white. To survive in an orphanage or the desert there can be no shades of gray. To him, you either lie about nothing, or you lie about everything. It's up to you to convince Adam that you're telling the truth this time."

"Sister, I want to find Adam. Will you help me?"

A smile crossed the lined face.

THREE DAYS LATER Sierra was back at the entrance to the Superstitions.

"Are you certain you should leave so soon?" Sister Delores had asked after taking Sierra to the bus station in Nogales. Luke had insisted on coming along and struggled manfully with Sierra's backpack and small suitcase. "Your arm still bothers you."

"It'll hurt no matter what I do. I don't want to wait any longer. I need to find Adam."

"You'll keep in touch?"

"Yes, of course. Thank you for going out of your way to help me."

"When I first came here, it was my job to help tend the children. Adam was one of my favorites." The older woman's eyes grew suspiciously bright. "Like Luke, he was once a happy boy. Before I die, I'd like to see that once more in the man.''

Sierra leaned forward and gave the nun a hug, then tousled the black curls on Luke's head.

"Goodbye."

Luke gave her a smile as the nun said, ''God's blessings on you both. Now hurry. You'll miss your bus.''

Sierra waved as the bus drove off. Craning her neck, she saw the old nun still watching, Luke standing close beside her.

The ranger at the sign-in entrance to the Superstitions was surprised to see her back. In fact, he almost didn't let her take the paint, which was still being kept in the holding pen. She'd called Weldon from the bus station, so she knew he hadn't collected his horse yet. He'd thought Adam might need the paint to search for his Appaloosa. But if Adam wasn't using Spot, why then, Sierra was welcome to do so.

"Adam went in by foot to look for his missing horse,'' the ranger told her. ''Why don't you wait for him here? I don't think you're up to riding with that arm,'' he said, nodding at her plaster cast and sling.

"Weldon gave me permission. Call him if you want. Besides, I grew up on a horse. I could ride with two broken arms, if you'd just help me saddle up. Weldon told me the paint's tack is in the horse trailer.''

"I don't feel right about this.'' The ranger hesitated. "I'd hate to see you back in the hospital.''

"If you won't help me, I'll saddle the horse myself. Either way, I'm going.''

When the ranger saw how determined Sierra was, he finally gave in. He first stowed her suitcase and backpack in the horse trailer's storage area. Then he saddled the paint, filled the canteens and even loaded the saddlebags with supplies Weldon had left behind.

"How long do you intend to be?" he asked anxiously, noting Sierra's wince as she mounted. "You only have enough food for a couple of days."

"As long as it takes for me to find Adam," she replied.

"For heaven's sake, be careful."

Sierra nodded and lightly kicked her heels into the horse's sides. They moved at a brisk walk through the entrance to the Superstition Mountains.

The day was overcast. Without the usual summer heat, Sierra was able to keep Spot at the same pace. She didn't see any thunderheads building as she rode deeper into the mountains, and for that, she was grateful. She'd be able to find Adam more easily if it didn't rain.

She didn't stop, not even to rest her arm, which was starting to throb and swell from the jolting of the horse. Sierra kept on a straight track toward Black Top Mountain. That was where the flash flood had occurred. Sierra was sure Adam would search for his horse there before moving on to the areas she needed photographed.

Her supposition proved to be right. At the end of the day she reached her destination. Sierra saw that someone had set up camp at their previous site. On closer inspection, she saw that the tent was Adam's.

He wasn't around, but Sierra knew he'd have to return before dark. She dismounted and awkwardly picketed the paint with her good arm. She'd unsaddle him later, when her broken arm felt a little better. In the meantime, she'd just rest for a while. Maybe she'd lie down in the tent if the sleeping bag was there.

It was even unrolled. Sierra sighed with relief as she tossed off her hat and stretched out. Thank goodness Adam hadn't taken the paint. She didn't think she would have had the stamina to hike in. She'd close her eyes, just to rest them, she decided. Within minutes she was asleep.

It was dark and chilly when Sierra awoke, but someone had covered her with her denim jacket, so the cold hadn't awakened her. The smell of cooking had. Her stomach growled. She hadn't eaten much of a breakfast back at the orphanage, and she'd skipped lunch altogether.

She got up, carrying the jacket outside.

"Sleeping Beauty awakes." Adam's words broke the stillness of the night. "Are you hungry?"

Sierra nodded, struggling to sling the jacket over one shoulder and insert her good arm through one sleeve.

"Here, let me help you." He rose from the fire and came her way. He shrugged out of his larger jacket and took hers. "Use mine. If you take off the sling, you can fit the cast through the sleeve. It's cold out."

Adam's jacket was warm from his body, and Sierra gratefully slipped it on.

"Thank you. But what about you?"

He draped her jacket over his shoulders. "This will do."

Sierra wished she could see his face more clearly in the flickering light of the fire. He handed her a plate of stew, but she wanted to talk first.

"Did you find your horse, Adam?"

"No, not a trace, just like I didn't find a trace of your tent or sleeping bag. The force of the water was too much, I suppose."

Just remembering how the flood had nearly swept Adam away, too, made Sierra's skin crawl.

"I'm sorry, Adam. Maybe you should have taken the paint to search. I know Weldon left him for you to use. You could have covered more ground, that way."

"More storms are predicted. That means more flooding. I don't own the paint, and I didn't want to take a chance with him."

"But you'd take a chance on your own life?" Her voice broke on the last words.

Adam's head snapped up at that. "You're hardly one to cry words of caution after everything you've done. Why did you come back, Sierra? To make sure I didn't escape with the treasure?"

"No!"

Adam's fork paused on the way to his mouth. "Don't look so surprised at the question. Why else would someone right out of the hospital come back here? You should be at the orphanage, resting. Instead you came racing back. Obviously you're more concerned with that damned mine than with your health."

"Adam, that's not true!"

"I saw you sleeping in the tent. You looked half dead, Sierra. Well, I'm afraid you came all the way out here for nothing. I was too busy looking for my horse and taking your pictures to worry about finding the Lost Dutchman."

"I don't *care* about the Dutchman," Sierra insisted. "I don't care if I never hear another word about the mine or its treasure as long as I live!"

"So you've said." Adam set down his plate, apparently finished with his meal.

"It's true. Even if I did find it, I'd trade it all to make that four-year-old my daughter."

Or to make you love me.

Adam wasn't quite convinced. "Why did you come back, Sierra?" he asked again, feeding the fire.

"Because I love you."

Adam glanced up. "We've had this discussion before."

"We didn't finish. You made me listen when I didn't want to hear. Now it's your turn to do the same."

"Why? It won't do anything except make things worse."

"Maybe it will, and maybe it won't. But I rode all the way out here to have my say, and I'm not leaving until I do."

Adam had stopped poking at the fire now. Sierra watched as he lit the small gas lantern. He placed it carefully on the ground, then came over and sat beside her.

"I'm listening."

"Believe it or not, I'm a very honest person. There's a reason—a very good reason—that I wanted a child badly enough to lie." She took in a deep breath, then blurted, "You see, I can't bear children. Ever."

To Sierra's astonishment, Adam didn't seem surprised.

"I wondered when you'd tell me."

"You *knew?*"

"I guessed," Adam said gently. "It seemed strange that a young woman would want to adopt so badly. Most women would be dreaming of having their own child. And then you were so touchy every time I asked why you wanted to adopt. It wasn't hard to figure out, Sierra."

Adam reached for her hand. His was warm and comforting, and she didn't resist. "How long have you known?" he asked.

"A year ago I was engaged, so it seemed prudent to see a doctor for a pre-wedding exam. I wasn't worried, as everything seemed normal enough."

"But it wasn't."

"No." Sierra sighed. "My checkup was a real eye-opener. The doctor did every test twice before giving me the bad news. No babies, no remedy and, finally, no wedding."

"Your fiancé left because of it?" Even the night couldn't hide the anger in Adam's eyes.

"Yes. I did suggest adoption. It honestly doesn't make any difference to me how I become a mother, as long as I can *be* one. But biological children were very important to Tony."

"Tony? Tony Miller?"

"Yes. We were engaged. When he heard about my sterility, that was the end of the relationship as far as he was concerned. He found himself a new fiancée, one who could give him 'the right kind' of children."

Adam's eyes narrowed at the cruelty of Tony's actions. "The man must be an idiot. Yet you're still working with him! Are you hoping to win him back?" he asked harshly.

"No, nothing like that! It's over, and has been for a long time. But then we were offered this book deal. The money was just too good to pass up. I needed it for the adoption lawyer and fees, and Tony wanted it for his upcoming marriage. The publisher wanted both of us, or no deal. So we agreed to do the book, then go our separate ways." Sierra stared into the darkness. "You don't know how hard it's been, working with a man who considers me defective merchandise.''

"Oh, Sierra . . . I'm sorry."

"Don't be. I don't have a complex about my problem. I may have lost a husband, but there was no way I was going to lose out on being a mother. I want a child, and adoption is the only way I'll have one.''

"That's why you lied to me about the Dutchman."

"Yes. Everything else I told you is true. I *do* love you, Adam. Even before that terrible flood came down the canyon, I turned away from the Dutchman. I gave up my dreams of fame and success—and adoption—to make sure you were safe. Adam, you have to believe me!''

"You risked your life, gave up your hopes and dreams, for me?" Adam's voice was hushed. "Sierra, why?''

"Because I want you alive. I want you to love me—as I love you.''

Adam brought her hand to his lips. "Sierra, I do love you. But there's no future for us.''

"Why?" The anguish of her cry made him wince.

"The desert, its people and its music—they're my life. But this isn't a life for you. Or for a child."

"I'll stay here with you. I love the desert," Sierra said frantically. "I never liked the cold. And even if this place was the North Pole, it wouldn't matter as long as I'm with you!''

"You're wrong, Sierra. It *would* matter. It's taken me a long time to overcome my childhood. I'd want my family to have a normal life. I couldn't offer that here. And I don't know if I could move back to the city. I tried that once, and it didn't work."

"But you said you loved me! We could find a way to—"

"No." The finality in that single word was devastating.

Sierra pulled her hand away. She stood up clumsily, her movements jerky. She couldn't, wouldn't break down in front of him. "I see. I think . . . I think I'll go to bed."

Adam stood up, too. "Take my tent," he said, almost brusquely. "I'll sleep outside."

"Fine," she replied, choking back the tears.

He pulled open the tent flap and they went inside. "Sit down. I'll take off your boots and help you undress."

Sierra sank to the ground with none of her usual grace. Adam removed her boots and socks, then slid his jacket from her shoulders.

Sierra felt the touch of his hands, and wondered if she could bear never feeling him, never seeing him again. The silence grew. Adam folded his coat, then placed it next to the saddlebags.

As though to break the silence, he said, "I finished taking your photographs and made some notes on the water holes. With the material you already have, you should be able to complete your assignment." He reached into his saddlebags and withdrew six rolls of film. "Your professional reputation will remain intact. All you need is a good courier service, and you'll be on your way. Shall I put these in your jacket?"

Sierra ignored his question. "It's because I can't have children, right?"

Adam thrust the film into the pockets of her denim windbreaker, which he laid on top of his own folded jacket, then blinked in confusion. "What?"

"That's why you don't want me. It's not because you live in the desert. You can't love me because I'm sterile."

Adam immediately sank to his knees and placed his hands on her shoulders. "You know that's not true."

"It is." Tears spilled from her eyes. "I should have guessed earlier. With your background, I'm sure you've had enough of orphans and orphanages. No wonder you don't want anything to do with me." Her voice broke, and she would have covered her face with her hand if Adam hadn't pulled her hard against his chest.

"You mustn't believe that!" He tipped back her face, but Sierra pulled her head away, eyes streaming. "Please don't cry, Sierra." His voice grew hoarse. He laid his cheek against her head and hugged her tighter. "Sierra, you're tearing yourself apart. You're tearing *me* apart..."

Sierra's good arm crept around his waist. This might be the last time she could be close to him! She pressed her lips to his neck.

"Sierra, don't." Adam tried to pull away, but Sierra reached for his hand. "I can't give you any commitment."

"Then just give me something to remember, Adam. Just give me love."

"Sierra..."

"Kiss me."

He did. Then they were stretched out on the desert floor, the sand receiving the warmth of their bodies.

At first Adam's movements were slow, almost tentative because of her injury, but then he grew bolder at Sierra's heated response. She did what she had wanted to do ever since the flash flood, when she'd almost lost him. She touched, she caressed, she loved. It seemed the more she had of Adam, the more she wanted. Even though she could feel his heart pounding wildly, his mouth against hers, she couldn't get close enough.

And then, suddenly, she was. Sierra gasped with pleasure at the beauty of their joining.

When it was all over, they lay in each other's arms, spent with passion. Adam ran his fingers lightly up and down her cast, as if the motion could heal the broken bones within. Sierra found the action strangely soothing.

"How's it feel?" he asked, continuing to stroke the white plaster.

"Like the rest of me," Sierra said, smiling. "Happy. Content."

Adam didn't reply at first. "Until you leave."

Sierra's blood suddenly ran cold, all traces of passion disappearing. "You'd still send me away?"

"Yes. Because I love you."

"Oh, Adam," Sierra felt her heart expand at the admission, then contract again. "We could make it work. We could."

Adam laid his fingers against her lips, silencing her. "You've heard my reasons. Let's just enjoy the time we have left."

Sierra couldn't bring herself to argue. Instead she snuggled closer to him in the dark. She had no regrets about tonight. If the short time they'd been together helped heal his past wounds, and hers, that was enough—for now.

CHAPTER TEN

THE NEXT MORNING Sierra awoke alone. She was disappointed but not surprised at Adam's absence. She dressed awkwardly, using only one arm, and was struggling with her boots when she heard the whinny of horses.

She hurried outside in her stocking feet. Adam had just thrown a spare halter on his Appaloosa stallion, and was slowly leading him into camp.

"Good Lord," Sierra breathed aloud. Lightning Bolt was a mass of gashes and gouges. His saddle was missing, his once proud mane and tail matted with mud and debris.

"It's a miracle this animal is still alive! Where did you find him?" Sierra asked.

Adam lifted the Appaloosa's feet one by one to check for damage before gently stroking his drooping neck.

"He found us. Heaven knows how he's survived, or where he's been all this time."

"He must have smelled Spot and found his way back," Sierra guessed. Horses were uncanny at finding other horses.

Adam nodded, caressing the raw battered muzzle of his horse. "The herding instinct is strong. If you hadn't come out here on the paint, I would never have found him. This horse couldn't have survived much longer. I have you to thank for him."

Sierra came closer to examine the stallion. "Except for this bad gash here—" she pointed to his left flank "—most of the external injuries seem to be healing."

"Yes, but I can't tell about internal damage."

"Do you think he'll be able to walk out?"

"He'll have to. There's no way he can be ridden, but he does have all his shoes. We'll take it slow and get him back to Weldon's. He'll need stitches for that gash. It looks bad, and it's still bleeding."

He switched his gaze to Sierra's feet.

"Speaking of shoes, you'd better go put yours on. The last thing we need is you stepping on a scorpion."

"After the flood, I'd be very surprised to find one," she said, but nonetheless she headed back for her boots.

A short while later Adam had fixed breakfast, packed the tent and saddled the paint. He helped Sierra mount up, then started walking, leading the Appaloosa by the picket line.

Sierra made several unsuccessful attempts to talk to Adam. In the excitement of finding the missing stallion and then the hurry to break camp, nothing had been said about the previous night. Apparently Adam intended to keep it that way. Finally, after her conversational efforts were politely discouraged for the third or fourth time, Sierra realized Adam was already pulling away from her.

After a long trek that lasted late into the evening, they finally reached the pass that would take them out of the Superstitions. The stallion had faltered a few times, but was able to walk into the waiting horse trailer. Sometime during their absence Weldon had dropped off Adam's truck and hitched the horse trailer to it. Adam helped Sierra down, then unsaddled and loaded the paint.

When the horses were ready, he came around and opened her truck door. "Where would you like me to drop you off?" he asked.

Sierra felt her heart contract. Was he in such a hurry to be rid of her?

"I thought I could go with you to Weldon's."

"No." He continued to hold open the door. "Once I get there, I'll be busy with my horse. You need to go home. I won't want to leave Weldon's until I know Lightning Bolt's okay. I have no idea how long that will be."

"I don't mind," Sierra insisted.

"Weldon doesn't have the room to put us both up."

"I can use the tent."

"With that arm? Don't be ridiculous. I'll call Phoenix to get you a taxi. If you hurry, you'll have plenty of time to finish your book."

Sierra drew on every ounce of pride she had. Lifting her chin, she climbed into the truck without another word.

Once inside Adam seemed to relent. "Sierra, I'd take you to the airport myself, but it's a long drive, and I need to get my horse to the vet. You do understand, don't you?"

"I only understand that you can't wait to see me go. After everything that's happened, everything we've been to each other—why?" She swallowed hard, trying to clear the lump in her throat. "Adam, don't send me away. Didn't last night mean anything to you? I love—"

Adam cut her off. "We need more than just love to build a future on, Sierra. You know that."

She bit her lip. "You have your music. Maybe you could . . ."

Adam sighed. "Sierra, I tried that. It didn't work."

"But you're composing songs."

"Yes, but they're for the reed flute. There's hardly a market for that, and certainly not for tribal songs."

"Surely you could do *something* with them," Sierra persisted.

Adam shook his head. "No. I told you, the songs have religious significance. They aren't for the general public."

"Then why do you learn them?" Sierra asked. "Just for your own pleasure?"

"There's that, and something else. I'm of mixed ancestry. I'm part Spanish, part Indian. Learning the songs makes me feel like I have some kind of heritage, a heritage apart from the Spanish orphanage I grew up in." He gave her a rueful smile. "Even if I don't know exactly what tribe I come from."

"Oh, Adam..." Sierra's throat tightened with sympathy.

He started the truck again with a savage twist of the key. "There's a campground nearby. We'll stop there so you can get ready for the airport."

Two hours later Sierra was showered, changed and standing next to a taxi.

"Here are your notes," Adam said. "I know you have Weldon's number. Would you call him and leave a message when you reach home? I want to know you had a safe trip and that your arm didn't give you any problems."

Sierra blinked back the tears and forced herself to take the notebook from his hand. She dropped it into her backpack, then awkwardly fumbled in her wallet.

"Here's my business card. I've written the address of my parents' ranch on the back. Will you keep in touch?"

"I don't want to give you any false hopes, Sierra." But he took the card.

"Things change. In the time I've spent here, they've changed for me." She watched as he slid the card into his shirt pocket. "They could change for you."

The stallion gave a pitiful nicker of pain, and Adam turned to look at the horse trailer. "I have to go, Sierra."

Sierra nodded. She handed the driver her backpack and small suitcase.

"I..." Adam hesitated. "I wasn't going to tell you this. But I did check out that location you had pinpointed for the Lost Dutchman. I didn't want you to risk coming back again."

Sierra couldn't work up any of the old excitement. It was all she could do to say, "And?"

"It *was* an old mine, but there was nothing inside except some rusty old beer cans."

"That's okay," she said dispassionately. "The way everything else has gone on this trip, I'm not surprised. It doesn't really matter, anyway."

"I thought you should know. If it means anything, I'm sorry."

Sierra nodded. "Thank you for looking. I wouldn't have been able to do it myself with this arm. I'm glad I know, anyway." She shrugged. "Well..."

They stood there, staring at each other. The taxi driver beeped his horn in impatience, then defiantly started the meter running to hurry her up.

Before Sierra could take the first step toward Adam, he threw his arms around her. He held her like a lifeline, and despite her cast Sierra wrapped both arms around his waist.

"You'll be roping again in no time. You take care of yourself," he said. "Make sure you see a doctor as soon as you get back."

"I will. Write me, Adam. Let me know how you are."

Adam swallowed, his eyes enfolding her even as his arms were letting her go.

"Goodbye, Sierra Vaughn." He gently urged her toward the taxi.

Sierra forced herself to get in. Her heart would surely have broken as she drove away, except for one thing.

The pain of loss on Adam Copeland's face.

SIERRA SAT in the doctor's waiting area. Her cast had just come off, and she'd been X-rayed to see if her arm had completely healed.

"Sierra? The doctor will see you now," the receptionist said briskly. Mrs. Vaughn, who'd driven Sierra to the clinic, gave her daughter an encouraging smile.

The doctor took one final look at the X rays as Sierra walked in.

"This happened six weeks ago?" he asked.

"Yes, in Arizona, during a horseback expedition."

The doctor shook his head. "Skateboards, motorcycles and horses. They all keep me in business."

Sierra was about to say she hadn't broken her arm falling off a horse, but then decided to let the error pass. She wasn't about to tell him the true story of her injury.

"And you're right-handed, too. That must have been inconvenient at work."

Sierra gave a noncommittal answer, not saying she was without work at the present. After making certain she and Tony met their new deadline, she'd told him they were finished for good.

"But, Sierra," Tony had protested, "we work so well together. I think we should seriously consider working on other projects."

"I wish you and your fiancée well, Tony. I really do. But frankly, I hope I never see either one of you again."

"You can't mean that! What about our book? It's due out on the shelves in six months! I'd planned for the two of us to promote it."

"You're on your own, Tony. As far as I'm concerned, you're a chapter in my life that's closed."

Sierra had left Tony, his mouth agape, without a backward glance. She felt no bitterness, no anger, just a feeling of relief. She even felt sorry for the future Mrs. Tony Miller.

The doctor finally finished his examination. "Well, Ms. Vaughn, your arm looks great. You needn't make a return appointment. Good luck."

She didn't need luck, Sierra thought to herself as she left the doctor's office. She needed Adam. In the four weeks she'd been back in Colorado, not once had she heard from him.

Sierra had given up her apartment in Denver and moved home to the ranch. She made a point of writing to Mexico and Arizona to let Sister Delores and Weldon know. Even then, no word from Adam.

So she forced herself to focus her energies on her family. Once they got over the initial shock of having her home, things settled into a surprisingly pleasurable routine. They all fussed over her arm, assured her the book would be a smash-hit best-seller, and did everything possible to make her feel at home.

Sierra was still waiting to hear about the *Southwest History* staff position. She didn't hold out much hope, but she had sent them a copy of the manuscript—a work that was a far cry from the unique and exciting book she'd imagined. Still, her phone calls to the magazine had assured her that a decision would be made soon. Sierra decided against looking for other work until then. In the meantime, her family spoiled her shamelessly.

Even Sierra's father joined in. He was forever urging his wife to cook Sierra the most delectable vegetarian dishes. Even her youngest brother, Jon, took time from the rodeo circuit to come and visit, shyly introducing his attractive new girlfriend. Her four sisters-in-law paid their respects, and the numerous nieces and nephews clamored around "Auntie Sierra" until the ranch literally rang with their laughter.

Sierra felt guilty for not having spent more time with her family. It shouldn't have taken an injury and financial problems to bring her home. That prompted her to admit to her parents how much she'd missed them—an announcement received with so much joy that Sierra finally put aside all her old fears about being unloved.

"You seem different somehow," her father had said one day.

"So—I don't know—at peace with yourself," her mother added.

"I've finally grown up." Sierra gave them a rueful smile. "What you must have gone through with me. I was a stubborn little brat, wasn't I?"

"No, you weren't," her mother contradicted. "You were just sensitive, that's all. Ranch life is hard, but it was harder for you."

"I hope you don't hold that against us," her father had said, and for the first time Sierra was shocked to see how old he looked.

"Oh, no, Dad." She thought of her roping skills, and how she'd been able to save Adam from death. "In fact, I want to thank you both for teaching me how to be strong."

Her parents' tearful reaction washed away the last traces of enmity between daughter and parents. Old relationships were strengthened, and everything would have been perfect if Sierra had only heard from Adam.

In desperation, she called Weldon in Arizona.

"I'm sorry, Sierra, but I haven't heard from Adam yet."

Sierra's spirits sagged at the news. "Have you received all the letters I've sent him, care of your address?"

"Yes, but Adam hasn't been around. Once his horse recovered, he left. I'm watching the horse, and I've got all your letters here unopened."

"Adam hasn't come back once? Not even to check on his horse? Weldon, where could he be?"

"I don't know, Sierra. I'm sorry. If I see him, I'll tell him you called."

Sierra tried Sister Delores in Mexico, receiving the same response. When she hung up the phone, even the nieces and nephews couldn't chase away her sadness.

Then, one surprising morning, Sierra heard some news that temporarily took her mind off Adam.

"Sierra!" her mother called. "Telephone. It's for you!"

Sierra hurried to the kitchen and snatched up the receiver.

"Ms. Vaughn? It's Mr. Rydell from the adoption agency."

"Mr. Rydell?" Sierra couldn't hide her astonishment.

"Yes. Ms. Vaughn, are you still interested in adopting?"

"I . . . Of course I am, but you said I wasn't eligible. I don't have a permanent job, and I'm in between freelance assignments at the moment."

"Actually, Ms. Vaughn, it appears you do. I took the liberty of calling the people you said had made you a tentative job offer."

"You mean *Southwest History?* Mr. Rydell, nothing is firm there, and in fact—"

"But it is. They assured me that although they aren't ready to make the announcement yet, the job is yours. I'd like to place you back on list, if that's acceptable."

Sierra's hand tightened on the receiver. "I'd love that, Mr. Rydell. But I have to be honest with you. If I do get this new job—"

"I understand it's yours."

Sierra couldn't take in the good news. "Then I'll be moving to Arizona. Is that a problem?"

Mr. Rydell tossed aside her worries. "We checked with our lawyer. It's not."

"I'll be working again by the time my name gets to the top," Sierra added, feeling a surge of excitement.

"That won't be necessary. We have a child for you right now."

Sierra nearly dropped the receiver.

"The little girl we'd originally planned for you went to the next people on the list. They'd hoped for a boy, but took the girl, anyway. I'm afraid things didn't work out for the couple or the child. Jennifer is quite timid and is frightened of men. The fact that her biological father is serving a prison sentence for assault probably has something to do with it. I think she might do better with a single female parent than a couple. If you're still interested, would you like to have her?''

''I can't believe it,'' she cried softly.

''What was that?''

''Yes, Mr. Rydell, *yes!*''

And Sierra became a mother, just like that. The paperwork and final interviews were rushed along, and four-year-old Jennifer became a Vaughn. Because of her background, the Vaughn men made an extra effort to reassure her. The child instantly attached herself to Sierra and quickly became comfortable with the rest of the family. Sierra fell head over heels in love with the little girl. Mothering came as easily, as naturally, as she'd always known it would.

Southwest History called before Jennifer arrived to confirm Mr. Rydell's news. She'd be starting her new job the following month. Until then, Sierra busied herself preparing for the move, and spending time with her new daughter and the rest of her family.

Yes, her days were delightful, but when she kissed Jennifer and put her to bed, her delight fell away. The loneliness began. Sierra wrote to Adam almost every night, long letters full of anecdotes about Jennifer, ranch life and her family. She told him, too, that she'd finished the book, and described her new job and her planned move to Arizona. In short, her letters spoke of everything except what she truly wanted to say.

That she loved him and missed him desperately.

All she could do was count the days until she and Jennifer left for Phoenix. She would search for Adam there; she had to—he'd left a hole in her life that couldn't be filled. Until then, she only hoped he was well, and that he was thinking of her, as she was of him.

If only he would call her, or write. But no letters or calls came.

Soon her letters no longer bothered to hide her love and longing for him. But still, no response. Sierra even started helping with the lighter ranch work during Jennifer's naps. She wanted to be so tired every night that she'd sleep heavily, without dreams.

It didn't work. And still no Adam.

By now her family knew what had happened between Adam and Sierra in the Superstitions.

"It's been almost a month, Sierra, and you haven't heard from him. Maybe you should stop writing those letters," her mother had timidly suggested. "They only make you sad. I hate to see you so unhappy."

Sierra hugged her mother, put on a brave face and sent her letters just the same.

Then it was almost time to move to Phoenix. Sierra's mother wanted to take Jennifer into the nearest town to make some final clothing purchases. Sierra would have loved to accompany them, but decided it would be easier to pack without Jennifer's eager "help." Instead she went with them in the car to the end of the long driveway, then got out, planning to walk back to the house.

"Bye, Mommy!" Jennifer waved from the window of the car.

Sierra smiled. She would never cease to feel that warmth when Jennifer called her Mommy. "You be a good girl for Grandma. I'll be waiting right here when you two get home," she called out.

The car drove away. Sierra gave her daughter one last wave, then started back up the driveway toward the house.

"She's a beautiful child. What's her name?"

Sierra whirled around at the voice. "Adam!"

He was there, on the road by the gates that led into the driveway. Sierra stared at him in disbelief, hardly daring to trust her eyes or the hopeful pounding of her heart.

He smiled as he walked into the driveway. "Surely her name isn't the same as mine."

"No, it's Jennifer." Sierra could barely get the words out. "Jennifer Marie Vaughn."

Adam stopped and nodded. "Jennifer. It's almost as pretty as Sierra." He moved toward her, but Sierra didn't wait. She rushed straight into his arms.

"Adam, Adam, is it really you?" she asked, head thrown back to meet his gaze. Her heart soared with hope as she saw not withdrawal this time, but welcome.

"It's me, Sierra. And please God, we'll never be apart again."

That was all Sierra needed to hear. She rested her head against his chest and cried. All the hours of loneliness dissolved under the healing power of those tears.

Adam held her even tighter, and his voice broke as he said, "Please don't, sweetheart. I'm sorry this is such a shock. I should have warned you I was coming." He lapsed into Spanish for the first time ever in Sierra's company and swore.

Sierra recognized the words and had to smile. "Adam, I know some Spanish." She wiped away her tears and looked back up at him with shining eyes.

Adam swore one last time, but in English. "Damn it, I came here prepared with words of romance."

"It's okay, Adam. You're *here*. I don't need words."

"Not that I have any right to say them to you."

"You do. You say anything you want."

But Adam still seemed angry with himself. "Instead, I end up cursing in words I thought you wouldn't understand."

"I've been around a lot of cattle-kicked men," she said, drinking in the sight of him. "And from you, anything sounds good."

"I should start over," Adam said at his most formal. "I want to say—"

"Adam, Adam, just kiss me."

And he did. The prepared speech was forgotten as their lips met again and again, filling the emptiness in Sierra's heart.

And still her heart demanded more. It wasn't until he said, "I love you, Sierra Vaughn. I love you more than I can say," that she gave a long shuddering sigh of relief and satisfaction.

Sierra kissed the corner of his mouth. "How did you get here?"

"I took a taxi straight from the airport. I only have the clothes on my back. I didn't want luggage to slow me down."

He reached for her hand, and they walked slowly up the long gravel drive.

"I'm so glad you're here." Sierra squeezed his arm again, not believing her good fortune. "It seems as if I waited forever." She thought of the time that had passed.

"It felt that way to me, too."

"Why didn't you come back sooner?" she couldn't help asking, despite her happiness. Their separation had been too long, too painful.

"I told you once before that I had nothing to offer you. After I left you, I headed back to Weldon's to take care of my horse. That's when the loneliness hit me. I wanted more out of life than sporadic contacts with friends. I wanted you.''

''Did you get my letters, then?''

''Yes.''

''But Weldon told me—''

''I made Weldon promise that if you called he was to say he hadn't heard from me. I didn't want you to build any false hopes...''

''Why didn't you at least answer any of my letters?'' Sierra cried.

He walked her over to an old tree stump and gently urged her down. ''I want you to know I read every one of them, Sierra. In fact, I kept track of you from the moment you left Arizona. I've talked to your father every week. I wanted to make sure you were okay.''

''But, Adam, I *wasn't* okay. I missed you dreadfully. No one ever told me you'd called!''

''I asked your father not to. For the same reason I told Weldon to say he didn't know where I was—not until I knew if I could make a living doing something beside guiding.''

Sierra's heart went out to him. ''These last months couldn't have been easy for you, Adam. I know they weren't for me.''

''With a future for both of us at stake, I had no other choice. Loving you, and not being able to offer you and Jennifer any kind of future—that was the hardest. A tent in the desert is no place for a family. I had to find out if music still offered me an alternative way of life.''

''You still should have called me. I would have understood. The separation would have been so much easier on both of us.''

Sierra's hand crept into his as they started for the house again.

"Sierra, I couldn't, not until I was certain I could offer you and Jennifer the best. When you pulled me out of that flood, you gave me a second chance at life. A woman like you deserves more than the life I could give you."

"A woman like me?" Sierra said with confusion. "What do you mean? I don't care what you do, as long as we're together."

"You risked your own life to save mine. As it was, you didn't escape unscathed. Your arm . . ." His voice shook. "I'll never forget that."

"A broken arm was nothing compared to your life, Adam. I would have gone into the water with you before I let that flood sweep you away." Sierra shuddered at the memory.

"I know." Adam stopped walking and turned her to face him. "That affected me more than anything since losing my adoptive mother. After you pulled me out, I knelt next to you and resolved to start afresh. I could only pray my new life would be worth sharing with you."

"A new life? With more than just . . . the desert?" Sierra dared to hope.

"The desert was my haven. But when you left, I realized I could never feel at home there again. Not without you."

"Oh, Adam. I feel the same way about anyplace you aren't." She hugged him, and then they resumed walking.

"I decided to do something with my music. I approached the Apache Junction tribal museum and they agreed to my proposal. In fact, they're as excited about it as I am. I'll be recording the tribal songs I've learned, and they also want me to do a study on cultural crossovers, such as Spanish musical influences on Indian melodies, and vice versa. It's fascinating work," he added with a smile of satisfaction.

"I'm so happy for you! So proud . . ."

"And there's more. I've started composing again."

"Adam, really?"

"Yes. I haven't composed much since I left the city. But then I decided to write some original pieces incorporating the musical patterns I've spent a lifetime learning." Adam grinned. "I think there might be a market for it, too."

"Oh, Adam! That's wonderful."

"You were my inspiration. Remember that song I played? It was my first composition in a long time."

He stroked her hair, his hand strong and sure, but Sierra looked up at him with troubled eyes.

"Adam, if you hadn't found work with the museum, would I ever have heard from you again?"

"I told myself no—but it would have been impossible. I lived for your letters. Each one made it harder and harder for me to cut you from my heart."

Sierra laid her face against his chest. "Adam, I had such nightmares. You don't know," she said, her voice breaking.

"I know, Sierra. Believe me."

They clung tightly to each other for a moment. Sierra was the first to lift her head. "When do you have to go back?" she asked.

"Far too soon. What about you, Sierra? Will you come back with me? Marry me? Start a new life with me?"

Deep joy filled her heart. "I'd go with you anywhere. Especially to Phoenix!"

Adam dropped a kiss on her forehead. "Congratulations. I should have said that earlier. *Southwest History* is in for a shake-up!"

Sierra laughed, a joyful sound.

"It all worked out, didn't it?" Sierra said. "Even without the discovery of the Lost Dutchman. The publisher was impressed enough with my original research to take a chance on me." She drew a deep breath. "Jennifer and I will be in Phoenix next week. After settling her in school, I was going to come looking for you. You weren't getting away from me so easily!"

"Are you sure you're ready to leave the ranch? You seem content here."

Sierra thought about that before answering. "I am, Adam, and so is my daughter. I've finally made peace with the past. It isn't anyone's fault I didn't fit in. My parents loved me and taught me the best they could. If it wasn't for ranch life, I wouldn't know how to use a lariat. You wouldn't be alive now. I can never repay my parents for that. Never." Sierra paused to take in Adam's dear face, then continued, "I have no regrets. I can always come back. In fact, I want to. They're my family, and now they're Jennifer's. But Adam, they can't fill the emptiness in my life. Only you can. The three of us will go back to Arizona together."

He took her in his arms again and kissed her fiercely. When he released her, he gazed into her shining eyes, at her smiling mouth, her cheeks flushed with joy. Then he brought both hands up to cup her face, his expression solemn.

"As long as you want me, Sierra, I'll never leave. I swear it."

"I won't ever ask you to leave, Adam. If you go, it will be because *you* want to."

"Then, my love, you'll never be alone again."

EPILOGUE

THE DESERT SUN beat down on the Arizona highway.
Despite the heat, the four people in the air-conditioned
family van were comfortable.

"Are we there yet?" Jennifer Vaughn-Copeland
asked her mother. "I want Luke to see our house!"

"We have a ways to go, yet, sweetheart. Don't worry.
Luke will see it soon enough." Sierra smiled at her
young daughter.

"Why don't you take a nap like Luke?" Adam asked
Jennifer in Spanish. Already Jennifer and Sierra were
both proficient in Adam's native language. "This is his
first day with us, and you've worn him out," he said
kindly.

"I don't want to take a nap, Papa," came the response. "I'm not tired."

Sierra and Adam exchanged a knowing look. The
excitement of picking up Luke from the orphanage had
been overwhelming for Jennifer.

"If you take a nap, we'll be home by the time you
wake up," Sierra told her daughter.

"Go ahead and try," Adam coaxed. "Please, for me,
Jenny."

Sierra smiled at the love in Adam's voice. Luke would
soon discover what Jennifer already knew. Adam was
the most indulgent of fathers. In the year since their
marriage, he'd spoiled Jennifer shamefully. Only the

little girl's devoted love for both her parents kept her disposition sweet.

Jennifer fretted, but since Papa had asked, she finally put her head down and fell asleep.

"She looks like a little angel. And Luke hasn't moved for the past half hour. I hope Jennifer gives her new brother time to adjust. I'm worried about him," Sierra said, for Luke's departure from his orphanage friends had been a tearful one.

"Luke will adjust, given time. The important thing is not to rush him." Adam reached for his wife's hand. "And he'll do even better without his new mother worrying herself to death."

"I suppose you're right. I just want everything to be perfect."

The love in Adam's eyes took her breath away. Sierra had learned that he used Spanish with her when he was most moved, and his reply was in Spanish now.

"It is, my love. Believe me, it is."

"Adam, please pay attention to the road!" Sierra urged. "When you look at me like that, I worry about your concentration!"

"As well you should," Adam replied, switching back to English, but he did as she requested. "We'll be home soon."

Sierra thought of the house Adam had built. They had taken the best of the modern world and adapted it to the starkness of the desert. The result was a comfortable home for the children, surrounded by the wide open spaces of Arizona.

At first Adam had insisted, for Sierra's sake and Jennifer's, that they live in the city, but Sierra had been just as insistent that they not. Neither her work nor Adam's required city dwelling. Adam would never be completely at ease with crowds, and Sierra would just as soon not share him except with close friends, like Weldon.

Jennifer was at home in both worlds, and that was as it should be. Sierra hoped to do the same for Luke. But she and Adam—all they needed was each other, and the privacy, the beauty, the memories of the desert.

"Do you want to stop at the Superstitions?" Adam asked. "We're almost near the turnoff for Apache Junction."

Sierra looked at the mountains in the distance. "I'd like to. We haven't been back since we were married."

It wasn't for lack of wanting. But since their marriage, Adam's and Sierra's days had been full. First there was Jennifer to take care of, and now Luke. Sierra had been quickly promoted at the magazine; the book had been a rousing success and her firsthand research of the previous year had led to some well-received articles about the Superstitions and their history. The professional acclaim she received was far beyond her wildest expectations. Her family and work happily filled her days, but left her too busy for desert camping trips.

Adam still went out into the mountains alone, but his trips were less and less frequent. His Indian friends now felt comfortable coming to visit Adam at his desert home, and Adam hated leaving his family. He, too, was a busy man; he was still working with the Apache Junction tribal museum, but his biggest success had come as an independent composer.

At Sierra's urging, Adam had renewed some of his music contracts. Now he was writing music that blended traditional Indian and Spanish patterns for a famous classical ensemble and his work was hailed as a breakthrough.

Sierra knew their present good fortune—and all the joy in her life—had been influenced by the Superstitions. "I'd love to stop," she said, "but should we? You know the children need to have dinner and go to bed."

"As do we, my love, as do we. And once we're there..." His next murmured remarks sent Sierra's pulses throbbing and put a blush on her cheeks. "A few minutes won't hurt," Adam said with a smile.

Her hand slipped back into his as the van bumped over the dirt road. Before them, the looming gold spires of the Superstitions rose from the desert floor. It didn't take long to reach their outskirts.

"Let's get out," Adam suggested.

"What about the children?"

"I'll leave the air-conditioning on. They'll be fine. We won't stay long."

Sierra nodded. They both got out and walked the short distance to stand at the foot of the mountains. The heat of the sun blasted their uncovered heads as Adam put his arms around her.

"It seems like another lifetime...."

"It was, my love."

Sierra gazed up at the Superstitions. "They're so beautiful. You know, Adam, I never see them without thinking of us."

"If you hadn't decided to write your book about this place, we would never have met." Adam's arms tightened around her.

"But I did, and here we are. Together."

"Yes. I think the Indians are right. This place has magic after all."

"Good magic." Sierra leaned against him. "I want us to come back here some day, when the children are bigger. Just the two of us, like the first time."

"Don't you think you'll be bored?"

"Bored?"

Adam smiled at the surprise in her voice. "What will you do without a treasure to hunt?" he teased.

Her eyes shone with joy as she turned to meet her husband's gaze. "I have all the treasure I'll ever need."

He lowered his head until their lips were almost touching. "Prove it," he said. And she did.

HARLEQUIN
Romance

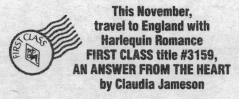

**This November,
travel to England with
Harlequin Romance
FIRST CLASS title #3159,
AN ANSWER FROM THE HEART
by Claudia Jameson**

It was unsettling enough that the company she worked for
was being taken over, but Maxine was appalled at the
prospect of having Kurt Raynor as her new boss. She was
quite content with things the way they were, even if the
arrogant, dynamic Mr. Raynor had other ideas and was
expecting her to be there whenever he whistled. However
Maxine wasn't about to hand in her notice yet; Kurt had
offered her a challenge and she was going to rise to it—after
all, he wasn't asking her to change her whole life . . . was
he?
